WHY
EDWARD
MORLEY
DIDN'T WIN
THE
NOBEL
PRIZE
IN PHYSICS

WHY
EDWARD
MORLEY
DIDN'T WIN
THE
NOBEL
PRIZE
IN PHYSICS

A FANTASY ABOUT SCIENCE

LES HARDISON

ARCHWAY
PUBLISHING

This story is pure fiction. The characters are real, historic figures, but the opinions and the ideas they express are purely made up, figments of the writer's imagination.

While they might have had thoughts along the lines expressed in this story, they would almost certainly have been intelligent enough to keep them to themselves.

Archway Publishing books may be ordered through booksellers or by contacting:

Archway Publishing
1663 Liberty Drive
Bloomington, IN 47403
www.archwaypublishing.com
1-(888)-242-5904

ISBN: 978-1-4808-1217-8 (sc)
ISBN: 978-1-4808-1216-1 (hc)
ISBN: 978-1-4808-1218-5 (e)

Library of Congress Control Number: 2014920262

Printed in the United States of America.

Archway Publishing rev. date: 2/2/2015

Contents

Acknowledgments

Without the help and encouragement of my daughter, Pat Jackson, I would never have completed this, nor would I have gotten any of the spelling or punctuation correct.

Thanks for everything, Pat.

PRELUDE TO A MEETING
IN JULY 1887

It was a warm, sunny Monday in July 1887 when Edward Morley finished his morning walk from his Cleveland home to

the entrance of Adelbert Hall at Case Western University. At forty-nine years old, Morley enjoyed the brisk walk when it was not raining and looked forward to another fascinating day. The walk always gave him uninterrupted time to think and to plan his day.

By far his greatest joy in life was in the completion of a carefully planned and meticulously executed experiment. He felt that his abilities as a scientist—a seeker of truth in a complex but consistent world—were at their peak. His second-most-interesting activity involved making sense of the data so lovingly and painstakingly acquired. This was the main task he and his friend and colleague Albert Michelson faced today.

It was generally accepted at the time that light was transmitted through space in the form of waves of some sort, although there was still some contention that particles of energy were somehow involved. The wave theory required a medium to conduct the waves, whereas the particle theory did not. But the experimental evidence for waves seemed overwhelming.

Some years earlier, Fizeau had constructed an interferometer to measure, not very accurately, the speed of light through a tube filled with flowing water. He, and most other physicists, expected that the light would move faster when it was moving in the direction of the water flow—with a velocity equal to that of the light through still water plus that of the water. This would be true if the light were passing through the liquid like a fish swimming through a stream, or if the light were made up 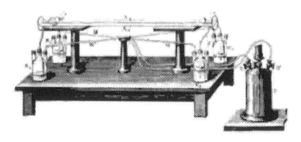 of particles, but not necessarily if the light took the form of waves. However, the light moved faster in the direction the water was flowing but not as fast as predicted, making the wave theory more promising.

While studying for two years in Europe, Michelson had tried to duplicate Fizeau's work and obtain a more promising result. He had designed his own improved interferometer and had it built. Then he had conducted some experiments with it that supported Fizeau's conclusion that light was a form of wavelike radiation. The interferometer had given more precise results than the rotating mirror method, and he had published some of these findings.

However, physicists were concerned about the medium through which light and other electromagnetic waves were propagated.

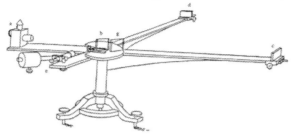

Michelson's 1881 interferometer

This medium, which was assumed to exist everywhere light could be transmitted, was called the luminiferous ether. It didn't seem to have any measureable properties other than the ability to conduct light. However, if it existed, it had to be moving with respect to the earth, unless we were, as the pre-Galileo astronomers thought, truly at the center of the universe. The velocity of the ether should be measurable even if nothing else about it was.

When Michelson had tried to use his interferometer to measure the speed of light both parallel to the motion of the earth around the sun and crosswise to that motion, he had not obtained results accurate enough to use as the basis for any conclusions.

After these unsuccessful experiments, he had returned to the United States and, in 1882, joined the faculty of the Case Institute of Applied Sciences as a professor of physics. However, the sciences were not the predominant field of study at Case, and he was not provided with a laboratory or financing for the building of one. Morley, on the other hand, had been working successfully in his chemistry laboratory at Case for some years

Morley, well versed in the current theories of light transmission but with less inherent leaning one way or the other, was inclined to defer to Michelson. This afternoon, hopefully, they would decide on the conclusions they would present with their description of the equipment, their experiment, and the measured results.

With these thoughts running through his head, Edward Morley climbed the three floors to his office and laboratory and prepared for his morning sessions with the undergraduate students.

THE 2 MEETING

The meeting with the photographer had gone well. Viewed from the standpoint of an outsider, the equipment was not as impressive as it was to the two men who knew the inner construction and the meticulous adjustments they had made to eliminate every error they could imagine.

But the photos would be impressive enough. The data, not the pictures, would tell the story.

They met for lunch promptly at noon. Both men, out of courtesy and concern for the digestion of the other, had spoken of the latest world news, like the Senate rejection of President McKinley's proposed annexation of Hawaii over the protests of Queen Liliuokalani. They also had discussed upcoming scientific meetings in general terms throughout their lunch.

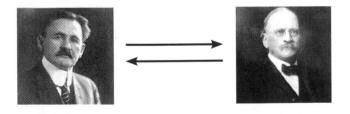

Not until the luncheon utensils had been put away and space cleared on Morley's desk did the two men get down to the real business of the afternoon, and then the following conversation took place:

MICHELSON. What in heaven's name are we going to tell the world we discovered during the past two years of hard labor, Edward? I am not inclined to say that we did all these experiments as carefully as we knew how and found out that what we were measuring doesn't seem to exist.

MARELY. I don't think we have any option but to lay our cards on the table. We made a good set of measurements, and what they tell us is that there is no difference in the speed of light when you measure it with or without the speed of the earth 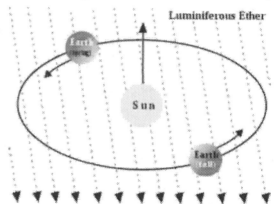 around the sun added to it. Let them draw their own conclusions. If we present this in the *Journal of American Science,* there will be many very brilliant men who read the results, and they may be stimulated in God only knows what direction to explain them.

MICHELSON. Well, we have done a lot of good work in the past, and we can well summarize where the inquiry into the nature of the ether stands at this moment, but it will rather look like we have subtracted from the sum total of knowledge than added to it.

MORLEY. I don't really believe that. I think we got good, re-producible results, which we should stand by. There are probably lots of ways of interpreting the results. For example, suppose that neither the particle theorists nor the wave theorists are right and that there is some completely different mode of transfer of radiant energy that no one has considered before.

MICHELSON. Surely you don't believe that, Edward. What could lead your mind in that direction?

MORLEY. We scientists always ought to keep an open mind and not let the things we have come to accept as gospel prevent us from considering absurdities suggested by our observations. We are sitting here in my office, seemingly at rest with respect to the universe around us, when we know we are moving at a velocity of eighteen miles per second around the sun. A few hundred years ago, this would have been considered an absurd idea and contrary to all of known science.

MICHELSON. I will grant you that, but still we have the hard fact of our data before us, and we must offer some sort of theory that would let us fit it into a logical frame-work; else we will simply have to say we failed to do what we started out to do.

MORLEY. Precisely what I am saying, Albert. We are obligated to put forward for consideration some alterative ideas that might explain the results if for no other reason than to give our colleagues some way to expand our understanding of the natural world.

MICHELSON. All right, let's follow your reasoning and presume that light is neither an electromagnetic wave moving through the ether nor a particle emitted from the light source. What in the world could it be?

MORLEY. Well, ignoring all of the generally accepted wisdom and looking at our data alone, I would first have to say that we have definitely measured the time required for the transfer of energy from a source to a receptor but that we did not measure anything about the path this transfer took through space or time.

It seems to me that light is so unlike anything of material substance that it may have some other way of moving from place to place than either undulating waves or moving by its own inertia like a cannon ball.

MICHELSON. I don't understand what you are talking about! What other way could there be that involves the finite velocity we have been measuring?

MORLEY. I'm just imagining right now. Probably the unimaginable.

But let's suppose, for a moment, that as the experiment proceeds, we—I mean our lab equipment, ourselves, and the whole universe—are moving through time. That is, time is a linear dimension like length, width, and breadth, but we can't picture this fourth dimension, because we, and our eyes and other senses, are bound within the three normal spatial dimensions at what we call the present moment.

Let me make a sketch on the board to illustrate my point.

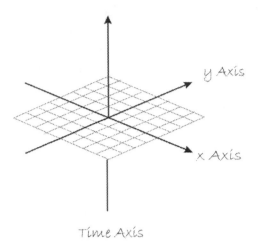

y Axis

x Axis

Time Axis

Morley's sketch of the universe as a flat plane moving through time

So the light leaves our source at one time and appears as if by magic at the receptor (our photographic plate) at a later time and a different place. Suppose the energy transfer from the source to the receptor were instantaneous. That is what it looked like to us in the laboratory. We measured the time between emission and the reception of the energy. We presumed that the light actually traversed the intervening space to our out mirrors and back to us during the elapsed time. But we also moved in the fourth dimensional direction during this interval. Perhaps we measured the distance we traveled in this time-like direction, and the light was transferred instantly. We might have measured the speed of the universe through time and not the speed of light at all!

Maybe we proved conclusively that light moves at infinite speed and that the universe is moving into a fourth dimension at 300,000 kilometers per second. This would fit our data perfectly, although it offends our preconceived notions of how things move through space.

MICHELSON. I see that it fits the data, but it flies in the face of all of the physical laws. There would be all sorts of ways this theory of yours could be tested and, I presume, disproved.

MORLEY. There certainly would be many ramifications. For example, if the three-dimensional universe is moving through a fourth, time-like spatial dimension, there are several ways it might be doing so.

If one used a two-dimensional analogue in order to visualize this situation, our three-dimensional universe would be represented by a two-dimensional surface where the distance is measured in time units like light-years. This surface could be a flat plane, in which case the universe would have dimensions that were constant with time. Or it could be a spherical surface, which would suggest that the distant galaxies are moving away from each other and from us. An expanding universe, you might say.

Or it could be going the other way, with the 3-D universe represented like a concave surface with the space getting smaller with time.

Astronomers might be able to tell us if this is happening at some time in the future.

And another thing. If light-energy transfer is an event that involves an emitting atom and a receiving atom, then what we are seeing right now must exist *right now* rather than in the past as we have supposed. The past and the future must be just as real as the present like the stations along a railroad track. We were at a station that is now in our past and are at a point along the track at the present but will come to the next station in the future. The past station and the future station are both real and continue to exist; we just aren't at either of them now. Marvelous where one's imagination can lead.

MICHELSON. I never heard such bosh! There is no question whatever that light is a form of electromagnetic wave. It has a measurable wavelength and frequency.

And what about that rot about the energy transfer taking place by magic? That is the least scientific thing I have ever heard you say, Edward.

MORLEY. Magic is that which is observed to occur but for which we cannot provide any acceptable physical mechanism. Perhaps I should have said "unknown physical phenomenon" instead of "magic," or "instantaneous transfer of energy."

But as I said, our data fits this model. Wouldn't it be great if we had actually discovered something new and exciting about the universe rather than just providing some sort of suggestion that the current thinking about light transmission is incorrect?

But this is your field rather than mine. I am just a humble chemist and should not be offering theories of optical physics. Suppose you provide some sort of satisfactory conclusion to our little mystery story.

MICHELSON. What you have convinced me of is that we should provide a good description of our apparatus, our experimental procedure, and the data, with only enough discussion to allow anyone who is interested in the field to come to the same conclusions we did. If the ether has any velocity, it was too low for us to measure it.

MORLEY. One more possible conclusion we should perhaps offer for consideration is that the ether is swirling all around the earth at phenomenally high velocities but that we have a small sample of it trapped here within our basement laboratory between solid brick walls, where, like the light we have been using, it can't get out.

MICHELSON. Enough! My head is beginning to feel stuffed with all this nonsense. I will start on a straightforward draft of the introduction, emphasizing the positive results we got previously in replicating the Fizeau experiments and the great increase in precision of the measurements we have made, and let the data speak for itself as you suggested at first.

MORLEY. Fair enough. It is your show, and I think your colleagues in the field of optics will have a true field day with it.

MICHELSON. Enough for one afternoon, Edward. Tomorrow I hope to have an outline, and we can start in earnest on our presentation of our data in a down-to-earth, scientific manner.

PRELUDE TO FURTHER EXPERIMENTS

Albert Michelson left Case Western for greener pastures in 1889, just two years after he and Morley had completed their apparently failed experiment aimed at measuring the velocity of the luminiferous ether (the medium which supposedly conducted light waves) and found the velocity as close to zero as they could measure.

Morley stayed on at Case, carrying his heavy workload and continuing to spend all of the time he could on research. He continued to be interested in the problem of how light moved through empty space if there was no ether to support the electromagnetic waves.

Also of concern to him was the theory put forward by George FitzGerald in 1889 and independantly by Heindrich Lorentz in 1892. This stated that the length of physical objects appeard to be forshortened in the direction of motion toward or away from the observer, because it took longer for light from the far end of the object to reach the moving observer than light from the short end. FitzGerald and Heindrich put this forward as one of the possible reasons Michelson and Morley had failed to determine the velocity of the luminiferous ether.

This seemed to be a possible explanation, and Morley was not one to leave a stone unturned in his experimental work. He felt he needed to eliminate the Lorentz-FitzGerald effect as a possible explanation for their conclusion that the ether was very nearly stationary relative to the earth.

Furthermore, Lord Kelvin, during a visit by Morley to England, had suggested that the thermal expansion of the sandstone base they had used for the experiment might have introduced some uncertainty into the results.

Morley took these possibilities to heart and, with the help of a physics department colleague, Dayton Miller, built and tested three more interferometers between 1900 and 1904. He hoped to obtain an even more precise measurement of the ether drift and that he might see something revealing in the very small differences in velocity the way he had in his experiments with the concentration of oxygen in atmospheric air.

The Morley-Miller interferometer, 1903

But these experiments, while considerably improved in precision, supported the conclusion that either the ether motion was very nearly zero relative to the earth or there was some mechanism that did not require a medium. The errors were not due to the Lorentz-FitzGerald contraction or the expansion or contraction of the apparatus.

Morley became more convinced with the passage of time that light transmission must involve some as-yet-undefined mechanism that he had inadvertently referred to as magic in his discussions with Michelson before the completion of their paper on the last and most well-known Michelson-Morley experiment. What could the mechanism be?

It was just after Morley had completed these experiments that Albert Einstein published his world-changing paper on what was to become known as special relativity. It was published in German on September 30, 1905. Although not immediately embraced as the answer to the puzzling behavior of light, it explained how, if you made certain assumptions, light could appear to move through a vacuum at a constant speed, c, regardless of the motion of the observer.

It did not provide any mechanism for the conduction of electromagnetic waves through the vacuum, so the conflict between the particulate and wave theories of light would persist, with each theory seeming to prove the other wrong. And Einstein's theory required some bizarre assumptions about the way space, time, and matter interacted.

In particular, special relativity (not Einstein's name for his theory), said that if a body were observed to be moving at a significant fraction of the speed of light, c, the physical dimensions of the body would shrink and disappear altogether if the object reached c. Further, the mass of an object would increase as the velocity increased and would become infinite at c.

All of this seemed to jibe with and reinforce the Lorentz-Fitz-Gerald theory even though Morley felt he had dealt with that as a possible reason for his experiments' failure to measure ether drift and had found no foreshortening of his equipment.

VISITING WITH MICHELSON, MAY 1906

Critical to this whole scenario was that the time a fast-moving body experienced would shrink so that moving clocks would run more slowly, giving rise to the notion that a future astronaut who made a round trip to a distant star would not age much if he went fast enough and might return to earth physically younger than his twin brother who had remained behind.

Finally and perhaps most importantly, the mass of a moving object would increase as its velocity increased, approaching infinity as the speed approached 300,000 km/s. These are all very counterintuitive ideas—actually bordering on the absurd—but necessary if you agreed with Einstein's premises.

But no one had a better approach. And no one had explained what it was that conducted the light though the vacuum in the absence of any luminiferous ether. The concept of fields—electric, magnetic, and gravitational—in space that oscillated to produce the waves that were transmitted seemed to Morley to be just as ephemeral as the ether, which he was coming to believe did not exist.

He thought it was time to discuss these things with his old friend and colleague Albert Michelson, who was now doing very well for himself as the first head of the physics department of the University of Chicago, a rapidly growing university funded by the Rockefellers. He wrote Michelson a letter suggesting they meet sometime shortly after Christmas in 1895 and discuss the matter further.

Michelson, who was doing well professionally at the University of Chicago but was not overwhelmed with social invitations, replied that he would be happy to see his old friend and coauthor and that they could both use some time away from the everyday work associated with the duties of their respective colleges.

So on a crisp, bright day early in May, the two old friends met in Michelson's office on the Midway on the South Side of Chicago.

MICHELSON. Morley, old chap. The years have been good to you. You don't look a day older than when we were inhabiting that musty old basement of yours at Case.

MORLEY. And you too, Albert. Though, for my own part, I feel a bit the worse for wear. The automobile trip from West Hartford was interesting but damnably long. If I ever do it again, I will take the train.

My, Albert, you have come up in the world. I dare say you aren't relegated to basement lab rooms these days.

MICHELSON. Hardly, but it is just as difficult to find the time, money, and space to do important things as it always was. There are so many more demands by all of these routine essentials than a good scientist should have to put up with.

But, Edward, let us get on with the business at hand and then go have a good dinner at my club and perhaps a spot of brandy afterward.

What is weighing on your mind?

MORLEY. Have you read Einstein's paper "The Electrodynamics of Moving Bodies"? It was published in German in September and has created quite a stir, with physicists coming down on both sides of the question. Has he hit the nail on the head or simply proposed an implausible, wild scheme to make our findings fit the theory?

Have you had a chance to review it and come to any conclusion on your own?

MICHELSON. Yes, I spent considerable time on the subject, but I have to admit that I did so at least partly because, now that I am a leading physicist at a major university, people ask me about it and expect that I will know what I am talking about.

MORLEY. And do you?

MICHELSON. Of course. I read the paper over from stem to stern and followed his very well-written argument—damnably well written for one so young. He doesn't even have his doctorate yet. But there seems to be no denying that he has found a way to explain the constancy of the velocity of light mathematically and come up with some startling conclusions as a result.

For example, he says that nothing can exceed the speed of light, because it would take an infinite amount of energy to do so. I never would have thought of that. And yet it gives me a bad feeling. How could the speed of material objects be governed by the nature of electromagnetic radiation?

Of course, the real headline conclusion of his paper is that matter and energy are different forms of the same thing. Really amazing, but I could find no flaw in his analysis.

MORLEY. That is certainly an understandable position and one I believe a majority of your fellow physicists have also adopted.

But I have a few points I would like to discuss with you. I still don't think he has considered all of the possibilities.

If you will recall, I wanted to include a speculation that we might have demonstrated that light was transmitted instantaneously and that what we measured was the speed of the universe moving through time. Or rather through a fourth spatial dimension at a fixed speed, which just happened to be c, the value we measured. Einstein simply ruled out that possibility, but his reasoning was not convincing enough for me.

And I am certain he has not found a mechanism for light to be propagated through empty space without any medium present to support wave action. The statement that the radiation produces fields in space is just a devious way of saying that it progresses through the emptiness without any mechanism at all—just as much by magic as in my explanation. Or lack of explanation, if you will.

No, I don't think he has hit the nail on the head at all. Not that I am, at this point in time, suggesting that we offer a more reasonable mechanism for the transfer of radiant energy than Einstein has offered—only that we continue to look for a mechanism that will fit all of the things we know about light.

I thought that you, who have devoted your life to studying light and have perhaps learned more about it than anyone else, might be able to fill this void.

In short, Albert, can you help me replace my magic with something a little more meaningful than "a hitherto unknown physical process"?

MICHELSON. It still seems to me that Einstein's step-by-step presentation followed very logically from his premises. Was there a fatal flaw in his reasoning?

MORLEY. I think there were two. First, he assumed that we had measured the speed of light in vacuo and rejected the notion that we had measured the speed of the universe through the time-like fourth dimension, although I am ashamed to admit we failed to include the speculation that this might be the case in our publications.

Second, he defined simultaneous events in a relatively roundabout way. He said two events are simultaneous if we find that they were recorded by two observers at some distance from each other at times differing by their local (but precisely synchronized) clocks by the exact time intervals equal to the distance between them and the event divided by c, the speed of light. That is, if we find that the observer closest to the event observed it at an earlier time than one farther away from it. Yet they would be simultaneous to Einstein.

The flaw here is that one cannot tell what is happening right now at any location other than that at which he, the observer, is located. All he can attest to is what he sees at the present moment, and I am inclined to think that everything he sees at the moment *defines* the moment. Simultaneous events are those that he can observe at the same moment as a single observer. Quite different from Einstein's definition, so the passage of time has to be treated differently than he did.

When I see two events occur simultaneously, it is because I see them both happen at the same time by my clock. They are simultaneous in my local time system, and this has nothing to do with what an observer at a different location would see.

Let me draw you a sketch.

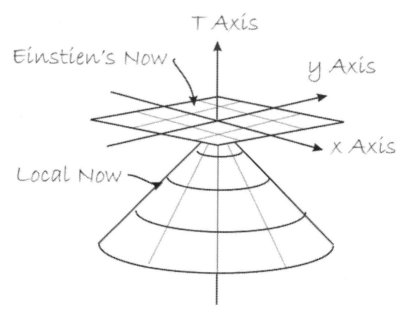

Morley's sketch of the universal and the local now

By Einstein's definition, the present, in which all simultaneous events occur, is the flat xy plane that represents our three-dimensional universe. But this is not true! It is the cone representing all of the things one can see at a given time that really defines right now. Any two simultaneous events have to occur such that I, as the observer, can see them at the same time in this local present.

In this local, present view of the universe, light travels from the source to the observer in no time at all, so far as the observer can tell—the magical transfer of radiant energy you taunted me about.

I maintain that, were we to postulate a mechanism that could account for the instantaneous transfer of radiant energy from a source atom to a receptor atom, our experimental results would make perfect sense. And Albert Einstein's theory would no longer hold water.

MICHELSON. So are you asking me to come up with your magical mechanism so as to debunk Einstein's spectacular theoretical treatise?

MORLEY. Yes, dear boy. If anyone could do this, it would be you.

MICHELSON. Do you have some sort of magical mechanism up your sleeve? Some hint as to how this might come about?

MORLEY. Only the vaguest of inklings.

MICHELSON. Tell me your vague inklings, and let me see if they suggest anything to me.

MORLEY. The only mechanism that would account for all the attributes we have measured for light over the years goes like this. Light has a characteristic frequency and seems to be emitted in discrete little packets. Einstein has called these packets photons. We never actually see light being transmitted through space and can only detect its presence when it falls on matter of some sort.

Contained in each atom, no matter what the element, there is an inner orbit containing a pair of electrons. These have an orbital frequency around the nucleus of the atom, and they orbit that nucleus at a particular frequency, which is determined by their temperature, ordinarily. The hotter atom has the higher frequency. But various forms of matter have different characteristic frequencies—like the sodium vapor we used as the light source for our experiments. I maintain that it is the kinetic energy of these inner atoms that we associate with radiant energy.

Were two atoms to be brought into juxtaposition geometrically so that the orbits were in the same plane and the centers of rotation lined up, the faster-moving pair of electrons would collide with the slower ones, transferring their velocity to the slow movers, and become slow moving themselves. The transfer of velocity, momentum, and energy from one atom to the other would have all the *measureable* properties of the transfer of radiation.

The receiving atom, supposing that the energy was now at a much higher level than the temperature of the atom would account for, would have to get rid of the excess energy by transferring it as kinetic energy to adjacent molecules, or by transmitting it within its own bulk volume by reradiation if the material was transparent or translucent, or by reflecting it as radiant energy in the visual light range, or as other forms of radiation. These transfers would comprise either absorption or reflection. They would encompass all of the known characteristics of light.

MICHELSON. Perhaps. Let me try to understand your picture. You have a two-dimensional universe with x and y axes on it where z is everywhere zero. A flat plane. Now two different times, by our local clock, are located by two such flat planes one above the other if the universe is proceeding in the upward direction. A material object moving from point A on the first plane to point B on the second plane actually makes its way step by step through the plane as the plane moves step by step through time. The path of AB is a straight vertical line if the object is stationary with respect to our coordinate system, but is slanted if it is moving and A and B are at different locations.

Thus, a fish swimming through water would actually traverse all of the points in the plane between A and B while in the plane representing the universe, which is moving through time.

But we have no evidence that light does this. We can't actually see a ray of light as it moves along. We can only see it if we interrupt the trip, in which case point B becomes a receptor in our eye.

In fact, it would fit our experimental model, both for the measurement of the velocity of light, c, and for the velocity of the ether being zero, if we presumed that the energy did, in fact, jump from the emitting atom to the receptor atom in zero elapsed time by the local clock of the receptor. There would be no requirement for ether to conduct the light through space, because it would not actually pass through space. It would bypass both time and space.

You just want me to provide you with a theory of how this could possibly be the case.

We would no longer have to look at the particle theory of light transference, as the energy would transfer directly from one atom to the other. The frequency of light would be the orbital frequency of the excited inner electron or electron pair that all atoms have.

You might, given a little time, be able to account for all of the observed qualities of light or any other radiant energy transfer via this mechanism if only you could get the emitting atom and the receptor atom to ignore both space and time and transact their business as though they were alone together.

MORLEY. Well said. I think you have the gist of my purpose for coming to see you.

MICHELSON. My dear friend, this all depends on defining your magic means of transfer of energy. Let me turn this seemingly absurd suggestion over in my mind for a bit and see if I cannot let my imagination best my common sense long enough to try to give you some sort of answer.

For now, let us put the weighty matter of how the universe actually works aside and tend to some more urgent business—namely, a good dinner at my club and that brandy we spoke of earlier.

So they adjourned for the evening and talked no more of Einstein and his theory.

They met twice more over a period of three days but did not make any progress toward a solution to the problem of how to support an alternative to the special theory of relativity.

MICHELSON'S 5 RESPONSE

However, after some three months' time, Morley received a letter from Michelson, which is reproduced in its entirety below.

Morley read Michelson's letter with disappointment.

Not only had Michelson sided with the young upstart Einstein, but he had apparently washed his hands of the matter.

Morley was no longer a young man with the energy and inventiveness he had once had. Still, he was tempted to contact his old friends at Case Western and propose to them that he return for a time with the objective of developing a program to define a rational theory of light transmission.

But no. Better to leave the science to the new, upcoming generation of physicists. They seemed to be filling the journals with increasingly complex and, to him, increasingly strange theories. His would not be among them.

August 18, 1906

Office of the Dean
Department of Physical Sciences
University of Chicago
5801 S. Ellis Avenue
Chicago, Illinois

Professor Edward Morley
Case Western Reserve University
Cleveland, Ohio

My Dear Edward,

I have spent some time considering your request
that I propose a theory of light transmission that
might satisfy your postulate—namely, that light
is movement of energy from one place and time
to another place and time without transiting the
intervening space or time interval.

This is a more intriguing idea than I had imag-
ined during your visit in January. Doubly intriguing, I might add, in that there is almost
no way to visualize any process taking place in
more than the three spatial dimensions we have
long considered to be the only ones that are real.

But as you pointed out, time does seem like a
fourth dimension, and our data would fit properly if the speed of light were taken as infinite
and the speed of the universe moving linearly
in this four-dimensional superspace were the
value c.

So I let my imagination roam freely. While I cannot picture it in my mind, there is no difficulty
describing this four-dimensional space mathematically. Now, were the expansion in the time-
like direction truly linear, an atom in three-dimensional space would truly occupy a contiguous position in space as its time coordinate

increased. It would, in reality, be a four-dimensional entity like a string stretching out from the past, through the present, and into the future.

But each of the locations in space would be firmly bound to a particular time. There would be no possibility of it overlapping a different location in space at a different time as your theory requires.

The only situation in which such atoms at different times and places could be expected to be contiguous would be if the progress of the universe through the time-like fourth spatial dimension were not linear in direction but were, instead, curled up tightly into a ball. This would require the existence of a fifth dimension. Which quite goes beyond the realm of plausibility.

But to continue my speculations, it would be necessary for what we think of as lines of sight in three-dimensional space to be wound like the strings on a ball of twine. Our location as an observer simply would lie somewhere far inside the ball with the past lying beneath us toward the core and the future outward from the core. This would place various atoms adjacent to each other although spaced at great distances.

So, while I can see the possibility of an argument that Einstein has it all wrong, on balance, I am inclined to accept his model, with the apparent inconsistencies, over ours. Although there don't seem to be any inconsistencies in your approach to the mechanism of energy transfer by radiation taking place instantaneously rather than by transmission of waves and the production of fields in space, we would have to come up with some way to prove by experiment the existences of the extra two dimensions beyond our own three.

So I am sorry, old friend, not to have been of any help.

Let's not forget your explanation, however, and perhaps someday the preponderance of evidence will turn in your direction over Einstein's.

My regards to you and your wife.

Yours faithfully,
Albert

6

MORLEY HAS SECOND THOUGHTS

The time was January 1910. Professor Edward Morley had retired from active teaching, and at age seventy-two, he had reduced his professional activities to following the rapid developments in physics and, in particular, the theories of transfer of radiant energy.

His last published paper, four years before, had described his continuing experiments to improve on the now well-known Michelson-Morley experiment aimed at measuring the velocity of the luminiferous ether relative to the earth. He and Morley had considered this earlier experiment to be a failure, because their data showed that the ether, so far as they could measure, had no velocity relative to the earth. This was the least likely of results even though they thought at the time that they had measured carefully and that their results were a good set of measurements although inexplicable in terms of the then-current state of knowledge of radiation physics.

They had discussed Morley's suggestion that alternative theories of the transmission of light and other forms of radiant energy might be required to explain their result, but Michelson had been content to present the data and let others provide the theory to explain them.

Michelson had, shortly thereafter, left Case Western University for a more prestigious position and not long after that had become the first dean of physics at the University of Chicago, where he still presided. He had continued experiments on the measurement of the speed of light and had worked toward perfecting better diffraction gratings for the improved definition of the absorption bands observed in light from the sun and the stars.

Michelson had, three years past, been awarded the Nobel Prize in Physics "for his optical precision instruments and the spectroscopic and metrological investigations carried out with their aid." The Michelson-Morley experiments were now recognized as a part of the foundation of special relativity as defined by Albert Einstein in 1905.

In 1907, just one year after his retirement from Case Western University, Morley had been awarded the Davey Medal by the Royal Society "On the ground of his contributions to physics and chemistry, and especially for his determinations of the relative atomic weights of hydrogen and oxygen." The lesser honor did not recognize his fundamental role in the Michelson-Morley experiment.

Unlike Michelson, Morley continued to be concerned that the transmission of radiant energy involved something more than wave theory modified, as Einstein had pointed out, to accommodate some phenomena that indicated that the transmission of light must have some particle-like properties.

In fact, light of a given frequency (color) was always transmitted in packets that had the same energy. Particles, however, would not produce interference patterns, suggesting that light could not be particulate in nature but must be wave-like.

However, no other form of waves exhibited the particle-like property of being unidirectional. One cannot imagine a wave moving through water but in a single, narrow beam of very short length compared to the distance it travels.

These questions continued to bother Edward Morley, and as a very careful experimenter who did not wish to leave any stone unturned, he had continued to work on experimental apparatus to remove any of the possibilities for error he and Michelson might have inadvertently built into their apparatus.

Just a few years before, about the time Albert Einstein was publishing the theory that later became known as special relativity, Morley and a colleague at Case Western had published a paper describing additional experiments with apparatus of his design, which provided much more precise results and removed some of the possibilities for error. His experiments indicated that the luminiferous ether's motion was zero with a much smaller margin of error than he and Michelson had measured.

His one qualification in the paper was that some colleagues had suggested that the motion of the ether, as it was being called, was only zero because the experiments were conducted in an underground basement laboratory. Perhaps there was a volume of ether trapped in the underground room that was motionless with respect to the earth, whereas that filling outer space could have any velocity whatever. He proposed to redo the experiments with the apparatus located on a hilltop.

However, his energy was not at the high level he had sustained for so long, and it appears that he did not carry through on his determination to remove all obstacles to accepting his and Michelson's data as conclusive.

So in his early retirement years, it still troubled him that they had been making measurement of something physicists were coming to believe did not exist—the luminiferous ether. And it troubled him even more that Einstein's theory was being accepted as gospel truth when it had, in Morley's view, numerous faults. In particular, he did not believe that the wave theory of light, however modified to take into account the limitation to the transfer of energy in quanta or photons, as Einstein had called them, was realistic. The transmission of light by waves that moved essentially through empty space with no medium present was just as magical as his proposal that the transmission of radiant energy was instantaneous.

Morley's home in West Hartford, Connecticut

MORLEY WRITES TO EINSTEIN

So in January of 1910, Morley decided to write to Albert Einstein and see if there could not be some clarification of the subject they both considered a key to understanding the way the universe functioned—a satisfying theory of radiant energy transfer.

Edward and Imbella Morley
26 Westland Avenue
West Hartford, Connecticut

Professor-Doctor Albert Einstein, Docent
University of Zurich
Rämistrasse 71
Zürich, Switzerland

January 25, 1910

Herr Professor-Doctor Einstein,

I beg your pardon for writing to you in English, but my German is both somewhat old fashioned and rusty.

Although we have not met, I have followed and admired your many contributions to theoretical physics over the past few years and believe they have been very great contributions to science and to our general understanding of the natural world. My own contributions have been considerably more limited, but you may be familiar with the experimental work published by Albert Michelson and myself that determined the speed of light in air to be essentially independent of the tangential velocity of the earth around the sun.

This has been interpreted by a number of physicists to demonstrate that the luminiferous ether presumed to be the medium in which light waves are transmitted does not exist. Others have suggested that we perhaps conducted our experiments in a basement room where the ether was trapped and therefore moving with the earth. And some, such as myself, are not satisfied that we have any sound theoretical basis to account for the observations.

Your theory provides, in the eyes of most concerned physicists, an explanation of how light can be conducted through space at a fixed velocity, which is apparently invariant and independent of the motion of the observer.

However, I have some questions with regard to your assumptions and would be most pleased if we could meet and discuss these matters.

I understand that such a meeting would, unfortunately, involve a lengthy ocean voyage for one or the other of us. As it is I who request the meeting, I should be happy to arrange for such a crossing if there is a date at which we might be able to meet for a few brief discussions.

I would, of course, prefer that such a crossing be made in the spring, when the Atlantic is less hostile to mariners than in the winter months and I should have less problem convincing Mrs. Morley to accompany me on a European vacation.

But I should be happy to visit you when it is convenient for you, if you feel it would be worth your while.

Most cordially yours,
Edward William Morley

Einstein answered promptly, allowing for the several-week delay in the delivery of the mail, in February 1910:

Professor-Doctor Albert Einstein, Docent
University of Zurich
Rämistrasse 71
Zürich, Switzerland

Professor Edward Morley
26 Westland Avenue
West Hartford, Connecticut

My Dear Professor Morley:

Thank you for your recent letter and your offer to visit me in Zurich. I appreciate your willingness to do so, as I am in the midst of all sorts of commitments and projects that I feel ill equipped to handle. Life was far easier for me while I was a simple patent examiner and not much was expected of me.

I have read both your paper done in conjunction with Albert Michelson and also your more recent 1904 paper wherein you repeated the experiments to measure the motion of the ether more precisely and to eliminate some of the possible sources of error in the previous experiments. I am happy that your results confirmed the earlier tests and lend more credence to the idea that the velocity of light is, indeed, independent of the motion of the observer.

This, of course, supports my contention that the light is transmitted through space as electromagnetic waves. I am curious as to your concern with the other assumptions made in the derivation of the equations that comprise my theorem. But we are always reminded that seekers of truth must keep an open mind.

I should be happy to meet with you, preferably during August, if this is suitable, on a date of your choice, provided you give me sufficient notice of your coming.

I look forward to meeting you and to discussing our mutual interests in the mechanism of light transmission through space.

Yours sincerely,
Albert Einstein

MEETING WITH EINSTEIN

True to his word, Edward Morley arranged a lengthy vacation for himself and his wife including a voyage out of New York sailing for London. There they would begin a forty-day tour of England and the Continent that would end on August 10, 1910, in Zurich, Switzerland, where they would check into the Hotel Storchen for a stay of one week.

On Monday morning, August 8, 2010, Morley made his way by carriage to the offices of Dr. Einstein at the University of Zurich. At 9:00 a.m. promptly, he presented himself at the office of the increasingly renowned physicist, whose name would later become a synonym for *genius* worldwide.

Albert Einstein

Morley was ushered into the office by a young man and briefly introduced. He was a bit surprised that Dr. Einstein's office and furnishings were relatively simple and not so lavish as even his own had been at Case Western University.

EINSTEIN. Welcome to Zurich, Professor Morley. I hope your trip has been a pleasant one.

MOREY. It certainly has, although there have been moments when one would rather not have been traveling. But it has been a memorable trip. We have seen so much and absorbed so much of the history of the Continent on our travels. I find your present location here in Zurich most magnificent. On previous trips to the Continent, I was attending to business and not at liberty to enjoy the countryside; the historic places; and, of course, the delightful people.

And I am grateful for your greeting me in English, saving me the embarrassment of conversing in less-than-elegant German.

But I must admit that the opportunity to meet you and discuss our common interest in the mechanism of radiant energy transfer was the motivation for the trip, and the recreational travel was simply the icing on the cake, as it were.

EINSTEIN. I am intensely curious about what you find in my work that would warrant such an expenditure of effort on your part. I see that you are no longer a young lad, to whom such a trip would be merely an adventure. I made every effort in my publications to define exactly what I meant by each and every term, starting

45

with what I mean by time and the simultaneity of two events. So far, there have been very few specific objections. True, there have been those detractors who claim that my postulates are wrong. Particularly, they say, that the velocity of light cannot logically be measured the same by one moving relative to the source and another stationary relative to the source, regardless of what the equations prove. But you and your colleague Michelson have demonstrated this to be true beyond a doubt.

MORLEY. Not exactly that, Dr. Einstein. What we did, and I think did adequately, was to demonstrate that when we made our measurements with the apparatus moving in the same direction as the earth's orbit around the sun and at right angles to the orbit, we measured the same speed for light emitted by our sodium vapor lamp. Now, we were not, at any time, moving relative to the source of the lamp with our measuring apparatus. The entire apparatus was, in any case, moving at the orbital velocity of the earth, varying only by the very slow rate of rotation of our circular table.

However, this isn't where my concern comes to the fore, because I agree with your conclusion, which is that no matter how you measure the velocity of light or any other radiation, you will get the same result whether the source of the light or the receptor is moving and no matter what you chose as your "stationary reference coordinate system." Of course, this only applies strictly to radiation transmitted through air, but it is not much different from radiation through a vacuum.

EINSTEIN. So where might there be a disagreement about the basic assumptions?

MORLEY. I have given this a great deal of thought over the years since we first ran our experiments, and I think the problem I have lies in the definition of what comprises two simultaneous events. As you said, you were most careful to spell out in detail what you meant by the word *simultaneous*. As I recall, you stated that two events were simultaneous if observed by two distant observers, each of whom noted the time of the observation according to his very accurate clock, and both then realized that their observations were made visually and that it took a finite amount of time for light to reach the observer, presumably at the velocity c. If the first observer were located x_1 units of distance away, his clock reading would have to be adjusted to an earlier time for the event. That is, if t_1 is the reading on the first observer's clock when he sees the event, then it must have occurred at an earlier time, t_1', such that

$$t_1 = t_1' + \frac{x_1}{c} .$$

Similarly, the same correction would have to be made by the second observer, so

$$t_2 = t_2' + \frac{x_2}{c} .$$

The events are simultaneous if, and only if,

$$t_1 = t_2 = t$$

and *t* is the true time of the event. I have paraphrased the discussion in your famous 1905 paper, but I think I have the sense of it correctly.

EINSTEIN. Precisely. You have summed it up very well. That is the core of my whole derivation.

MORLEY. Well, this is a precise definition, but it defines time as the time read on two individuals' clocks when they are separated by some distance and their clocks are synchronized, so they always define *now* exactly to be the same time.

By your own standards, these two cannot see each other at the instant this simultaneous event takes place; nor can they communicate in any way during their observations, unless, of course, they happen to be standing at the exact same location, at which point they might be considered a single observer. What you have defined as *now* for both observers is the time at which their clocks both read exactly the same, and in order to do so, you have to presume not just that the speed of light is invariant with direction but also that it is, in fact, the well-established value of c—300,000 kilometers per second or so.

EINSTEIN. I must agree with all you have said so far. Still, I find no reason to disagree with anything in my definition of simultaneity.

MORLEY. You have defined *now,* the present moment, according to both observer's clocks and made a convincing argument that each of them cannot see anything else that exists in this moment because of the time required for light to make its way from any distant object to an observer's location; he can only observe things that are in his past.

I think there may be another equally logical way of defining simultaneity that is a bit more intuitive, which is, to my view, equally useful.

I would prefer to define *now* as all objects and events that I can see or communicate with by means of radiation of any sort at a given time on my clock. They are what I can see right now.

As an observer, it is all I can attest to at the moment by my own nearby clock. I have no direct way of observing anything in the universe as it is *now* by your definition. At any time, I can look around me in all directions and see objects both very near, like my clock, and also objects that are very far away, like the moon and the stars. By my own direct observation, this is all of the world that exists at the moment. If I choose to define this moment in time as *now,* all I am able to see (or, by analogy, communicate with by electromagnetic radiation of any sort) exists at my present time, t_1. Another observer viewing the same universe will define his time, t_2, to be exactly the same as mine, but what he sees will be different even though our clocks are synchronized.

By my definition, two simultaneous events are two events that I can see happening at the same time. How far away they are does not matter. That is, were you to light a candle standing next to me, and were I to see a distant star transformed by a nova as you did so, I would call these simultaneous events simply because I saw them at the same time. And I wouldn't care what an observer distant from me said about their times of occurrence.

I am pleased to see that you have a chalkboard in your office, which will make things easier to explain.

If I see a stationary object at a distance x removed from my observation point, I can calculate the time that would be shown on a clock at that point. It is simply

$$t_1 = t_1' + \frac{x_1}{c}$$

or

$$t_1' = t_1 - \frac{x_1}{c},$$

if you choose to call a distance in the opposite direction a negative distance.

From this, I could calculate the time a second observer would view this same object simultaneously by taking

$$t_1' = t_2' = t'$$

and setting

$$t_2 = t_2' + \frac{x_2}{c}.$$

However, our two clocks, although now synchronized with each other, would not agree upon the time of this event. However, there should be no difficulty in

translating observations made in reference to the proposed frame of reference to those using your definitions
of simultaneity and the passage of time.

It is necessary to recall that we are simply applying our
manmade definitions to the physical things we can observe and measure and trying to make sense of them
as best we can. What I have described is the situation
in which I feel we found ourselves when we did the
experiments that failed to show any velocity for ether
drift. It made me consider what we knew at the time
and what we didn't, and we did not have your insight
into the relativity of time in making the measurements.

I thought at that time that there was another possibility
to account for our observations that would not require
a medium for the transfer of radiant energy through
space, which involved the possibility of a fourth spatial dimension with characteristics of time but rather a
length dimension proportional to the passage of time. I
called this T, a spatial dimension, to distinguish it from
t representing time, so

$$T = ct.$$

If I could make a sketch for you of my condition of the
relationship between *now* as you defined it and *now*
according to my definition, it would look like this:

Here you see a three-dimensional picture representing
our three-dimensional universe as a flat plane with x
and y dimensions but z taken as zero everywhere. Instead of the z dimension, we can now show a fourth
dimension, which I have called T, representing the path

our universe moves along as we move from the present into the future. Thus both the plane, which I have called "Einstein's now," and the cone beneath it, which I have called "local now," are both moving upward from the past into the present and going toward the future.

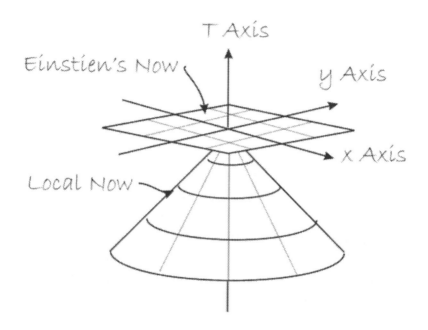

Repeat of the figure drawn for Michelson

What I can see is that if $T = ct$, then our experiments make perfect sense. We measured the speed of the universe moving into time at the rate of 300,000 kilometers per second. If you take this as the correct interpretation, then what is the actual speed of light? It is obviously infinite, as I sense the velocity of radiation of any sort in my local now this same local time it is emitted. That is, there is no time of transit of the light or radiation through space in the world seen by the local observer. And we can be no more than local observers.

Of course, if the speed of light is infinite, there is no question as to why all observers, no matter where located or how moving, would get the same result if they used a method like ours to measure it. They would all be measuring the speed of motion of the universe into the future, which we may have proved is the same in every direction.

Were you to accept that the speed of light is actually infinite, at least as observed by my definition, our data would fit perfectly, and there would be no need of a medium for the conduction of radiant energy through space.

You can see that this alternative approach to the interpretation of our data would have all sorts of ramifications and open many doors for reinterpretation of some of the conclusions based, in part, on our experimentation.

EINSTEIN. Whew! That is a great deal to consider.

My initial reaction is to say that there seems to be no room in your approach for electromagnetic radiation through space, and there is so much evidence that such radiation does, in fact, take place that I will approach your alternative with perhaps an aspirin tablet or two this evening and see what comes to me.

But I think we have done far more for a first session than I had anticipated and suggest that we meet again tomorrow, and you can take me further into your theoretical picture. I am sure you have much more to tell.

MORLEY. Sir, I did not really intend to go so far in the introduction to my thinking today, but when you opened the discussion of simultaneity, I just got carried away.

Thank you for your most gracious audience.

EINSTEIN. Shall we meet in the afternoon tomorrow? I am going to be tied up all morning with academic matters.

MORLEY. Agreed. I shall be here at 2:00 p.m.

A SECOND MEETING

They did meet the following day, Tuesday, at 2:00 p.m., and were both well rested and prepared for another discussion of Morley's theories.

Einstein was not as eager for the discussion as Morley, as he had experienced innumerable previous discussions with both learned physicists and laymen who had quarrels with his papers. For the most part, he had been only mildly defensive, feeling quite confident that he had presented his ideas in a workmanlike manner and had labored long and carefully over the manuscripts of his published papers so as to leave as little open to question as possible.

However, Morley was talking about a whole new perspective on time—new to Einstein's own whole new perspective on time. While it did not strike him as likely to hold water when carefully analyzed, he respected Morley's scientific acumen and knew of his reputation as a meticulous experimenter not known to reach hasty conclusions. And he was curious about what sort of arguments Morley could summon to back up his odd notions about time.

So they met and chatted amiably about the trip, and the remarkably good weather, and the recent upsurge in interest in the basic physics of the universe, which was in part due to Einstein's remarkable papers.

EINSTEIN. Good morning, Herr Professor Morley. I trust our alpine air helped you sleep well?

MORLEY. Of course it did. I don't know when I have felt so vigorous in the morning. I chose to take a brisk walk from the hotel rather than call a carriage, and I found it most invigorating.

When they had exchanged pleasantries, they got down to the business at hand.

EINSTEIN. I am sure you have much more to tell me this morning about this theory of yours that time is constant along one's line of sight rather than throughout the universe. But first let me tell you how I admire those of you, and particularly yourself, who have the talent and intelligence and persistence to do experimental physics.

I was not a particularly good student while I was an undergraduate at the university and had a good deal of trouble with some of the laboratory courses. I was quite good at absorbing the theoretical portions of the lectures, but ach! When we were assigned to duplicate one of Galileo's or Newton's experiments in the laboratory and determine the magnitude of the gravitational constant experimentally, it was a different story. I was all thumbs. My measurements were inaccurate, and it was almost painful for me to plod through the exercise when I knew perfectly clearly what the answer should be.

Meanwhile, many of my classmates managed to carry out the assigned experiment with apparent ease and reached conclusions that coincided quite nicely with those who performed them originally.

Rather than viewing them as competent mechanics able to do things carefully and accurately with apparent ease, I thought of myself as lacking in some fundamental trait that might doom me to failure. However, in time, I found that I was good at interpreting some of the results the careful experimenters obtained and could sometimes see in these results some new or heretofore-unnoticed correlation or relationship.

So I am having some success as a theoretical physicist with no laboratory at all assigned to me, as I am not expected to make measurements competently. Rather, I am totally reliant on the experimental physicists to provide grist for my mill, as it were. And I am truly grateful to you and the many others who generate the hard data I have the privilege of thinking about. You, my dear Morley, are the epitome of the diligent and productive experimental physicist.

When you published your well-known paper with Michelson, I was impressed with the originality of your work and also with your workmanship and ingenuity. I would never have been able to undertake and complete such a project.

But I was even more pleased with the presentation of your data in its full detail and with a minimum of speculation as to the unexpected and somewhat hard-to-believe result. I very much admire your persistence in continuing this work after Dr. Michelson had moved on to greener pastures.

MORLEY. Thank you for those kind words, Dr. Einstein. I have, as you indicated, spent the bulk of my lifetime working to measure some of the physical properties of the world we live in, perhaps in more meticulous detail than was required, but I have been satisfied with most of the results. And for the most part, I agree with your approach—that is, believe the data and question the conclusions drawn from it.

As I was gaining an education, although it was primarily in chemistry rather than physics, I too noted the difference in the affinity of some students for the practical side of laboratory work while others seemed more inclined to the comprehension of the theory.

One of my instructors pointed out to me as an adage something he had learned by observation of those who worked, as I did, carefully and diligently to gather data. He said it was his usual experience that when someone did an experiment, he was most likely to produce very good and reliable data. However, when he drew conclusions from the data and tried to explain why it came out as it did, there was much less reason to have faith in his analysis, because that was not where his skill lay.

EINSTEIN. But still, though I took none of the data I used in my analysis of the relationship of space, time, and motion, I too am in the group worthy of suspicion, as I was a drawer of conclusions. So you are quite right to question them. And, of course, I may also be suspicious of yours.

You presented an argument that, rather than living in a world I defined as what exists at this moment, which is exactly the same moment for each observer no matter where located in the universe, each of us has his own private universe consisting of what he can see or sense at the moment from his unique location. Surely, you cannot convince me that the world at this moment in time is not the real world as I have defined it.

MORLEY. Nor do I wish to convince you otherwise. What I am saying is that we, as physicists, do not have any access whatever to any other part of your real universe at the present moment. Rather, what we see is a different one, which I called the local universe, and it is in reference to this local universe that we make all of our measurements. It is in this universe that we have measured the speed of light and the speed of all other objects moving relative to our position, which we always regard as fixed.

EINSTEIN. This is an intriguing concept. You have obviously been thinking on it for a great deal of time, so what has the acceptance of your premise led you to believe that is different than I might expect?

MORLEY. Well, sir, it led me to believe that our data on the speed of light might be in error. Mind you, I am not suggesting an error in measurement but rather an error in interpretation of the data.

If you grant me that what I see at the moment comprises the world in which I make my measurements, you must conclude that the speed of transmission of radiant energy—light—is infinite. Do I not register the eclipse of the sun by the moon, where both lie along one of my lines of sight, as beginning just as the orbit of the moon intercepts and blocks the first rays of sunlight? You would hold that that event occurred about a second earlier than I became aware of it. I should retort that, according to my local time, it happened as I saw it. To believe otherwise, I would have to make a correction to my actual observation based on your definition of time.

I should then counter that your definition of time is based entirely on experimental evidence, all of which has been gathered by observers who made observations just as I did.

EINSTEIN. But this is, on the face of it, an absurd conclusion. How can you possibly account for the progress of waves through space without any time elapsing? And if you did not measure the speed of light with your experiments, what, then, did you measure?

MORLEY. I have some thoughts in that direction, and I think we might have measured the rate our universe is moving through a fourth, time-related dimension. Just as in the sketch I drew for you yesterday, which I see you still have on your chalkboard.

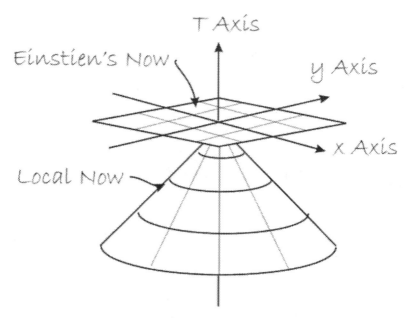

Morley's sketch, repeated

I do not want to overstate my case here but simply to point out that this is an alternative interpretation of the data that should be examined with some care.

EINSTEIN. So your speculation is that the universe is moving in this fourth dimensional direction at the velocity c, yet light essentially races ahead of it, moving from an earlier time to a later time infinitely faster.

MORLEY. True, and our experimental data fit very well into this pattern. For consistency, I will call this the local time scheme, and the alternative, using your definition of simultaneous events, the universal time scheme.

In the local time scheme, one measures distance in a variety of ways, but the simplest of them is if there are markers of some sort like mileposts with smaller subdivisions in between that the observer can count. These are fixed in space, and they are stationary with respect to the observer. That is, they represent distances away from the local observer. So objects can be located relative to these local markings, and one can tell by visual inspection of the surroundings how far away the object is.

Because an object is observed to be stationary, it does not imply that it was always so, so it is best to presume that the measurement of velocity, and the determination that the velocity is zero, be limited to a relatively short time interval. Thus if we say, "I see an object at a distance of ten kilometers at the present time," that may be entirely true when the object is an automobile parked by the roadside. Yet minutes later, it may be moving with a finite velocity with respect to the observer.

It is fairly obvious that an object that is stationary with respect to the observer at a distance x would also be located at a distance x from the observer using the universal time system. However, it is a different story for objects moving with respect to the local observer.

Are any of my definitions causing any concern in your mind, Dr. Einstein?

EINSTEIN. No, Edward, if I may use your given name, as it seems we shall be at this for some time. Your presentation has been quite clear so far. Please continue.

MORLEY. Well, sir, we were getting to the crux of the situation, where my observer observes a moving object and wishes to determine the velocity of it. He does so by making two measurements of the position of the object at two times according to his clock. Preferably, these measurements are made over a very short interval, during which the velocity of the object is presumed to be constant.

For purposes of discussion, we may call the time interval $t_2 - t_1$, or Δt. Ideally, this would be a very, very short time interval, which we might represent by dt, representing an infinitesimal time interval. The difference in measurements of distance at the beginning and end of the period can be taken as Δx, presuming that the object is moving directly toward the observer, or the infinitesimal dx, corresponding to dt. The velocity is then

$$v = \frac{dx}{dt} \cdot$$

Mind you, this is an observation made in reference to the local observer's visual observations taken at his local time.

Our immediate task at hand is to determine how this should be translated into a velocity in reference to the universal time system as you have defined it.

We can do this step by step as follows.

Let us presume that the corresponding velocity relationship in the universal time system is

$$v' = \frac{dx'}{dt'},$$

which is just the same, but the primed terms refer to the universal time system.

Now, it is apparent that

$$v' = \left(\frac{dx'}{dt'} \right) = \left(\frac{dx'}{dt} \right)\left(\frac{dt}{dt'} \right)\left(\frac{dx}{dt} \right),$$

where the last term is simply v, the value measured by the observer using his local time system.

So

$$\frac{v'}{v} = \left(\frac{dx}{dx'} \right)\left(\frac{dt'}{dt} \right).$$

Now, the distance measurements may be presumed to be made over the same distance of travel in reference to both time systems, so the first term in parenthesis is one. In this case, the times measured will be different, and the geometry of the situation is such that the second term is the ratio of the elapsed time in the universal system divided by the elapsed time in the local system at which the starting and ending events defining the time period are measured.

The relationship that satisfies this condition is simply

$$\frac{dt'}{dt} = 1 + \frac{v}{c}.$$

You may satisfy yourself that this expression, simple as it is, is true for the conditions I mentioned, and you can also derive it a number of ways from the geometry of the figure I drew on your chalkboard and the assumption that the motion of the universe in the fourth dimensional T direction is at the velocity c.

From the geometry of the situation, it is evident that

$$\frac{v'}{v} = \frac{dt}{dt'} = \frac{1}{1 + \frac{v}{c}}.$$

The ratio of these velocities will always be one when the observed velocity is zero and will be less than one when the measured time is greater than zero. If the measured velocity becomes very large, approaching the infinite, the value of v', the associated value in the universal space-time system, will approach c.

The velocity that is measured from a single observation point must always be corrected by this ratio when the results are to be expressed in terms of universal time.

Paraphrasing Jesus, this is my rock, and upon this rock I will build my case—the case that this, and all I have been able to derive from it, fits the data Michelson and I obtained and leads to some further startling conclusions.

EINSTEIN. Bravo! You have made an excellent presentation, but you have called upon me to suspend my belief in the fundamental basis of radiation theory and believe that light is transmitted instantaneously by your magic process.

I will have to spend some time thinking this over and see if there is any way I can realistically entertain such a notion.

MORLEY. Thank you. One does tend to become glib about a subject to which one has given a great deal of thought and to get carried away when one has an opportunity to expound to so receptive an audience.

I only ask this of you as you mull over what I have said. I have defined a concept of time that is realistic in that it is what we experience and what we can attest to. So there is no problem in defining it as the basis for a coordinate system. In reference to this coordinate system, light of all frequencies does appear at the eye of the beholder at the same time (by the definition of the system) as it leaves the emitting radiation source.

I have not violated any rules in setting up my coordinates, and you may retort that in the real universe, light continues to appear to move at the velocity c.

EINSTEIN. True enough. We are all intent on creating a model of the universe that behaves the way we see real objects and the occurrence of real events, and we do not question the reality of them. It is only our model that requires scrutiny. I will try to keep this in mind.

As to meeting again, I have some pressing matters to attend to on Friday morning. Will that fit your travel schedule?

MORLEY. I have booked passage on the *Lusitania* out of Portsmouth for August 20, and it will take a full two days of travel by rail with connections to reach there in time for the sailing. That means that my wife and I shall have to depart on Monday, August 17, at the latest. But I think I can conclude the presentation of my thoughts on Friday and perhaps a short time on Saturday if you can spare the time.

We can, of course, correspond by mail beyond that date if necessary.

However, I feel that a man with your grasp of the sciences will have no trouble deriving all of the equations I have done—I dare say overnight, whereas it has taken me several years of thought and effort.

EINSTEIN. You sell yourself short, Edward, and please call me Albert. I shall do my best to set aside my prejudices and see where your premises take me.

Until Friday, then, auf Wiedersehen!

THE THIRD MEETING
WITH EINSTEIN

Einstein and Morley convened again on Friday, August 14, for a third discussion of Morley's interpretation of the data he and Michelson presented in 1897. Morley had confirmed this data with further experiments and published it in 1904, shortly before Einstein's paper on special relativity explained how light could apparently pass through a vacuum at an invariant speed regardless of the velocity of the observer with respect to the source.

In the earlier meetings, Morley had made several points with which he expected Einstein to agree.

First, Morley and Michelson had not measured the speed of light as constant regardless of the velocity of the receptor relative to the source, as their source and receptor had moved at essentially the same velocity during all their measurements. They had no means for measuring the velocity of light from the sun as they were moving toward it or away from it during the measurements.

Second, there was an alternative to explain the measurements they had made while attempting to detect the effect of luminiferous ether drift on the speed of light—that is, that they had measured instead the velocity of the universe moving in a fourth-dimensional spatial direction that human beings sensed only as the passage of time.

Third, they had made all the measurements visually using the time at the position of the receptor of the energy emissions they were dealing with. They had made all these measurements on the presumption that the universe at each moment in time consisted of what they saw at that moment. That is, they saw the universe at their local time as the present universe, not as a collection of radiation sources in the past. This formulated a local time system as opposed to the universal time system spelled out so carefully by Einstein in his 1905 paper.

Finally, if one relied upon the observations made by an observer using his local time, it was necessary to correct them if one wished to use them as though they had been measured somehow by magic in the universal time frame. The correction factor was simple:

$$v' = \frac{v}{1 + \dfrac{v}{c}}.$$

The reason the velocity appeared slower in the universal time frame was that time differences must be assumed to be larger values to place objects and events at the proper location in space and time according to

$$\Delta t' = \Delta t \left(1 + \frac{v}{c} \right).$$

These corrections put a different light on the derivations contained in special relativity, as Einstein's theory had come to be known.

Today, Dr. Einstein was expected to have had time to consider the presentation of Dr. Morley and to have some comments. Because time was running short for Morley, they got down to business very quickly.

EINSTEIN. A very good morning to you, Edward. Sorry, but it does occasionally rain in Zurich. I hope it did not greatly inconvenience you.

MORLEY. Not at all. I am accustomed to taking my daily constitutional in West Hartford, rain or shine, and a serviceable umbrella is always with me.

I am anxious to hear what you have to say in response to my admittedly outrageous proposal that there is a different kind of time system altogether that we are forced to use when doing experiments.

EINSTEIN. You made your points quite clearly and convincingly. However, they all revolve around your postulate that light can actually move from place to place instantaneously, which leaves one at a loss to explain what mechanism could be responsible for such a phenomenon. But your line of thought was sufficiently interesting that I attempted to put away my inherent tendency to discount the possibility or your being right and to look at how that would affect the conclusions I drew in that 1905 paper.

And I must say that the conclusions were sometimes in agreement with my positions and sometimes poles apart from them.

Let us start with the conclusion that nothing can go faster than the speed of light. I said, as I recall, that it was because it would take an infinite amount of energy to accelerate any body with a finite mass to the velocity of light, because the mass would increase as the velocity increased and become infinite as the velocity approached c, the speed of light.

You would agree that nothing can move faster than the speed of light simply because the velocity would become infinite if it did, and there would be no need to postulate that mass increased with velocity. In other words, Newton's laws of motion would hold without correction at very high velocities. Is this conclusion correct, Edward?

MORLEY. It certainly is.

EINSTEIN. Then I should have to say, "Score one point for Dr. Morley," as simplicity is always preferable if it is not in error.

Likewise, when one body is moving relative to another, and that body is moving relative to a third, I would contend that their velocities should be added as vector quantities. But the result would only make sense if the velocities were corrected by the same factor I used to correct the mass of an object being accelerated relative to the stationary observer. That is, each velocity should be corrected by the factor

$$F = \sqrt{1 - \frac{v^2}{c^2}} \ .$$

Otherwise, a spaceship, no doubt piloted by a species vastly superior to man, moving at the velocity of 0.6c relative to the earth, which dispatched a second spaceship, starting at zero velocity relative to the first and accelerating to 0.6c relative to the first, would of necessity be going at 1.2c relative to the earth; and we both agree that nothing can exceed the speed of light, c, using my coordinate system.

However, you would say that if the measurements were made by observers living in your local time system, they would be seen as going more rapidly than they really were in the universal time system but that their velocities would be directly additive after the proper correction factors. Is this true?

MORLEY. After a fashion. It appears to me that the velocities would be directly additive if they were all measured in the local system with respect to the same local observer. However, the observer on earth would always see both ships as moving farther away from him in space and would therefore be seeing them farther and farther in the past by universal time while they remained visible to him in his local time and therefore in his local present.

If you use my premises, each velocity would be corrected to the proper value to be expressed in universal time by multiplying the observed velocity by

$$\frac{1}{1+\dfrac{v}{c}},$$

not by

$$\sqrt{1-\frac{v^2}{c^2}}.$$

These terms do not differ much at ordinary, everyday observable velocities, but should man succeed in bringing material bodies to very high velocities, the differences would become significant. Perhaps, someday, we may be able to accelerate small objects to such high velocities.

If I am not mistaken, the real observer sees the first spaceship moving at a velocity of 1.50c rather than 0.6c. The second spaceship, moving at o.6c relative the first in universal terms, would be at twice this speed, or 3.0c, relative to the stationary observer. It would appear to the pilot of the first spaceship to be moving at 0.6c if he referred it to universal time. Thus, in the local time system, no velocity contraction factor is required. Velocities are simply additive as vectors and follow the Newtonian laws without correction.

But the real problem here is how the spaceships could be accelerated to these high velocities without the expenditure of an infinite amount of energy. Your theory is that the velocity cannot approach the apparent speed of light, c, because the mass of the object increases as its speed relative to the observer increases.

The idea is that the mass of an object is not a real physical property of the object but rather a property that may change as the observer moves away from or toward the object at high speed.

I do not think this is a necessary conclusion. Rather, I believe that the mass of an object and its position in space at any given time (by whichever time system) is an immutable property of the object. Velocity, on the other hand, is dependent on the reference system chosen, and all of the properties of the mass that are derived from the velocity also have meaning only relative to the observer.

I have worked out the correction that should be applied to the acceleration determined by the observer using his local time observations and found the correction to be

$$a' = \frac{a}{\left(1 + \dfrac{v}{c}\right)},$$

where a is the acceleration based on measurements made referenced to the local observer's clock and a' to the corresponding values translated to the universal time system.

I will, with your permission, indicate my derivation of the relationship between observed and calculated accelerations on your chalkboard during our recess.[1]

EINSTEIN. Quite intriguing! Do continue.

---

[1] This is shown in Appendix to Chapter 10, for anyone who in interested in following it.

MORLEY. So I maintain it is not the mass of the object being accelerated that must be corrected to make a proper translation from the local system used for measuring accelerations but instead it is the calculated values of the acceleration that require correction.

This finding is at such odds with your theory that I hesitate to bring the matter up for discussion for fear of being offensive.

EINSTEIN. My dear Edward! We are seekers of truth, not political rivals for elected office. We need not consider ourselves as contestants in a life-or-death struggle but as fellow workers trying to make sense out of an enormously complex problem of how to construct a theoretical model that actually works like the real universe around us.

Both of us must be prepared to accept the truth from the other and, if necessary, to abandon our fondest theories. I certainly am willing to consider this and could do no more than apologize for having let my thinking go astray if this is the case. You too must be willing to bend to the preponderance of evidence, if need be.

So please go on with your presentation, and we will consider that, so far, it makes good sense, assuming that your basic postulate is true—that is, that light can go from one time and place to another time and place instantaneously.

MORLEY. I must compliment you on your open-minded approach. I fear that I may have, myself, become more biased than is proper toward the theory I have spent so much time with.

But before we continue, let me reiterate that the reference system I have postulated, where events are simultaneous when I see them occur at the same time, is the time frame we as experimenters actually use. We have no alternative.

On the other hand, when we see a moving object and identify its position at a given time by our reference clock, we cannot know with any degree of certainty where it is at the same time according to the universal reference system. We must take on faith that it will continue at the same velocity and along the same path for the necessary time period between our observation and the time when the universal clock moving along with the object reads the same time as our clock now reads.

EINSTEIN. All that you say appears to be true, and it is a most interesting concept. As you say, it runs totally counter to my own approach to explaining the invariance of the speed of light.

But right now, it is not my objective to defend my position as though we were members of a debating team each assigned to defend his position. My sole aim right now is to understand what you are proposing as an alternate theory and to see if it continues to make sense.

So before you proceed, let us take a respite and then come back to your further conclusions.

MORLEY. Excellent. I continue to applaud your open-minded-ness. I am not sure I would have reacted with the same generosity.

Let me conclude by saying that we have established a method for translating velocity results measured with respect to the local time of the observer into the pre-ferred framework of reference for physicists through the ages and that this has led to a similar method for translating measurements of acceleration of objects from our local time frame to the commonly accepted universal time frame that you, Albert, have so meticu-lously defined.

Einstein responded that there was no experimental evidence that this alternative theory was the right one, and Morley responded that there was no experimental evidence that Ein-stein's interpretation was right either. In particular, his own experiment, the Michelson-Morley measurement of the motion or lack of motion of the ether, was evidence that there was no medium for the conduct of light from one place to another. To Morley, that suggested that the invention of electric and mag-netic fields was simply another way of explaining the magic transfer of energy from place to place without any medium for conducting it through the intervening space.

Appendix to Chapter 10

Derivation of Acceleration Correction

Starting with

$$a' = \frac{dv'}{dt'},$$

differentiate the velocity as it would be calculated for the universal time system with respect to the passage of time in that system. This is relatively straightforward, as we know the relationships necessary to translate both velocity and time values measured in the local system to the correct values for the universal system. The universal system velocity v' is obtained from the measured local velocity v by

$$v' = \frac{v}{1 + \dfrac{v}{c}}.$$

To obtain the acceleration that can properly be used in the universal space-time system, it is first necessary to determine the derivative of the universal velocity with respect to the local time, and then correct the time to the universal system.

So, v' must be differentiated with respect to time in the local system using the derivative of a product, according to

$$\frac{d}{dt}(xy) = x\frac{dx}{dt} + y\frac{dy}{dt}.$$

This yields

$$\left(\frac{dv'}{dt}\right) = \frac{d}{dt}\frac{v}{1+\dfrac{v}{c}} = \frac{\dfrac{dv}{dt}}{\left(1+\dfrac{v}{c}\right)} - \frac{\dfrac{v}{c}\dfrac{dv}{dt}}{\left(1+\dfrac{v}{c}\right)^2} \, ,$$

which reduces to,

$$\left(\frac{dv'}{dt}\right) = \frac{\dfrac{dv}{dt}}{\left(1+\dfrac{v}{c}\right)^2} = \frac{a}{\left(1+\dfrac{v}{c}\right)^2} \, .$$

Now,

$$a' = \frac{dv'}{dt'} = \left(\frac{dv'}{dt}\right)\left(\frac{dt}{dt'}\right) \, .$$

The final correction factor is

$$\left(\frac{dt}{dt'}\right) = \frac{1}{\dfrac{dt'}{dt}} = 1+\frac{v}{c} \, .$$

Combining the factors.

$$\frac{dv}{dt'} = \left(\frac{dv}{dt'}\right)\left(\frac{dt'}{dt}\right) = a\left(\frac{dt}{dt'}\right) = \frac{a}{1+\dfrac{v}{c}} \, .$$

$$a' = \frac{a}{1+\dfrac{v}{c}} \, .$$

QED

THE DISCUSSION WITH EINSTEIN CONTINUES

MORLEY. So it is apparent that the acceleration measured in the local time system by the local observer must be reduced in magnitude to find the apparent acceleration in the universal time system.

For a velocity of zero, the measured acceleration is used without alteration in the universal frame of reference and is also zero.

For small velocities relative to the value of c, the correction is trivial and would be unnoticeable for objects with ordinary velocities experienced in everyday life. For example, if the velocity were less than 0.01c, the acceleration in the universal system would be 0.99999 times the measured acceleration.

However, at a measured velocity of c, the acceleration would have to be reduced by a factor of eight, and of course as the velocity became infinite to the local observer the acceleration would be reduced to zero for the universal system of coordinates.

Of course, in the local time system, there is no theoretical limit as to how fast a material body can be moved through space relative to the observer. However, it seems unlikely that the velocity of any physical object would ever reach the value of c, which would translate to the universal time system as c/2, or half the speed attributed to light. Light itself alone seems to reach beyond this presumed barrier, but I do not believe it is forced to move through space and time in the ordinary way, as I have said before.

EINSTEIN. Again, we come to the crux of the problem with your approach. What means of transport is there that is not limited to passing through the traversed space?

MORLEY. So far, we have confined our discussion strictly to measurements of distance and time that can be determined by an experimenter and, under many circumstances, repeated by another to ascertain that the measurements are valid. When we talk about the method of transport of light, we are, of course, venturing into another realm completely.

No one has ever observed a ray of light in transit. We can only detect the transmission of radiant energy when the transmission process ends and the light has already ended its journey. But I think we have strayed from the concrete here to the more esoteric. I would like to get back on path.

The most sensational line of your 1905 paper was the equation that is the simplest, namely

$$E' = mc^2.$$

I would, for consistency's sake, use E' for the symbol to suggest the possibility that it might be different from the corresponding value of energy calculated by an observer in the local system, should he be able to perceive the velocity of the universe in the fourth-dimensional direction. I did not use primes for the mass and apparent velocity of light, c, because it seems that these should be independent of the system of measurements.

I find this equation to be very nearly in keeping with my own devious approach,

$$E = \frac{mc^2}{2},$$

based on the simple kinetic energy equation we inherited from Newton and differing from my own value solely by the inclusion of a reciprocal of the square root of two in the velocity my derivation.

However, our conversation has suggested to me that there might be more truth in your version than mine. But I must first explain why I feel that there is enormous energy associated with matter, which is common to all matter in the universe and essentially unchanging with the passage of time. This energy is not directly measurable, but it seems to follow from our experiments that, if the velocity of light is not identical with the value c, then it must have been the velocity of the apparatus in this fourth-dimensional direction that we measured. Thus this energy relates to transport in a fourth direction, which is not directly detectable.

I can explain how the experimental results could be so interpreted, but that is a digression from the matter now at hand. I think you may be right about omitting the square root from the denominator but based on other considerations, which I hope we have time to get to later in the day.

TRANSLATION 12 EQUATIONS

MORLEY. While I have come to believe that mass is a property of matter independent of its velocity and invariant with time and location in space, this is not true for velocity, which is quite dependent on the motion or lack of motion of the observer. I should call the velocity a relative quantity, as one must define the location of the observer at the time the observation of position is made. Velocity may change with time but also with changes in the velocity of the observer.

Similarly, all of the quantities involving velocity are also relative ones. These include acceleration, momentum, energy and force.

All of these have straight-forward formulae for translation of observed values (or quantities derived from observed positions and times). Again, I have used primes to designate the quantities after translation to the universal time frame.

These formulae are

$$\Delta x' = \frac{\Delta x}{1 + \dfrac{v}{c}}$$

when the distance is measured over the same elapsed time in both systems and

$$v' = \frac{v}{1 + \dfrac{v}{c}}$$

for the case where the distance traveled in both systems is the same and the time interval is measured—or for the converse case, where the distance interval is constant and the time required to traverse it is measured.

In either case, for momentum:

$$P' = \frac{P}{1 + \dfrac{v}{c}} \; ;$$

for kinetic energy, where:

$$E' = \frac{m_0 c^2}{2}\left(1 + \frac{v'^2}{c^2}\right) = \frac{m_0 c^2}{2} \cdot \frac{\left(1 + \dfrac{v^2}{c^2}\right)}{\left(1 + \dfrac{v}{c}\right)^2} = \frac{E}{\left(1 + \dfrac{v}{c}\right)^2} \; ;$$

for mass, which is invariant in the local system and equal to the rest mass, but which increases with velocity in the universal system:

$$m' = m_0\left(1 + \frac{v^2}{c^2}\right) = m \; ;$$

for acceleration:

$$a' = \frac{a}{\left(1 + \dfrac{v}{c}\right)} \; ;$$

for force:

$$F' = m'a' = \frac{ma}{\left(1 + \dfrac{v}{c}\right)^2} = \frac{F}{\left(1 + \dfrac{v}{c}\right)^2} \; ;$$

and for work, or rate of energy change with time:

$$W' = \frac{W}{\left(1 + \dfrac{v}{c}\right)^3} \; .$$

These equations all derive from simple arithmetic operations, but one must be careful to keep the definitions of time and space in the two systems properly sorted out.

In summary, all of the measurements of relativistic parameters made by an observer and referenced to the time on his clock when he observed the event can be converted to the universal system you defined by simply dividing the observed value by the ratio of time in the universal system to time in the local system.

The exception to this rule is the mass, which does not vary with velocity in the local system, but must be presumed to do so in the universal system of measuring time.

These equations differ significantly from those you described in in your famous paper on relativity, yet all of them produce consistent results when measurements made in the local universe are recalculated to apply to your coordinate system, where events are simultaneous only if the synchronized clocks read the same time.

EINSTEIN. I must say I admire the symmetry of your derivations. I see that you state the equivalence of the two methods of measuring velocity, but I will have to withhold judgment for a moment to convince myself that this is true.

It will take me a few minutes of concentration to ascertain that your statement is accurate. Please excuse me for a moment ...

Aha! Yes, you spoke correctly. The two methods of measuring velocity are equally correct, and they do lead to the same values.

13

A SECOND OBSERVER

EINSTEIN. But, of course, these derivations all depend on the existence of a single observer whose location in space and time is exactly the same in both systems. It does not take into account that a second observer moving relative to the first would have a completely different set of observations and therefore a different set of velocities to use in these corrected values.

MORLEY. Surely, but if the second observer was in the same location as the first, his observations would be identical to those of the first observer. However, were the second observer moving relative to the first, his perception of most of the variables necessarily would be different.

I believe that the properties of the moving object that are special to the object and should be measured as the same regardless of the motion of the observer are only the mass of the object and its location in space at any given time. I believe these are, at any time, independent of the motion of the object or the observer.

However, all of the kinetic properties of the object are totally dependent on the relative position of the object as it traverses space and time. That is, the velocity, acceleration, momentum, and kinetic energy are all measured relative to the observer in question. None of these properties can be expressed except in relative terms. The velocity, for instance, cannot be described as one hundred meters per second without defining the reference system, which is generally assumed to be fixed, although there is no reason to assume the reference system may not be moving with respect to yet another arbitrarily fixed reference system.

EINSTEIN. What other tricks do you have up your sleeve, Edward?

MORLEY. Well, I had fits, I will admit, in dealing with the proposition that light travels equally well in both the positive direction and the negative direction in the universal plane so that an observer at the origin can see or be seen by a second observer at a distance. The two observers do not see each other at the same time, though, either by your definition or by mine.

Yet in the local time frame I have depicted, light seems to be able to travel only toward the observer from objects that lie in the vertically disposed cone that defines his present. Light leaving the observer's position can only travel upward in the $x = T$ or $-x = T$ directions, forming a cone that defines the future locations where a second observer could see the primary observer.

EINSTEIN. Again, you have given me a lot to digest, and I would prefer to sleep on the subject matter and respond to it in the morning.

Have you anything more to add today?

MORLEY. I am overflowing with ideas and conclusions and had only hoped to be able to cover a few of them in the time you have most generously granted me. If your schedule for the day permits, I would like to cover two additional points. The first is the matter we left hanging about the missing factor or two in your remarkably insightful E=mc² equation.

I have, in my proposed local coordinate time system, considered only the kinetic energy of matter, which I have always supposed to be

$$E = \frac{mv^2}{2}.$$

In my local system, I have presumed that the measured value c from my experiments was simply a velocity like all others, and when we presumed ourselves to be "stationary", our mass would have only the energy associated with moving at the velocity c in the fourth dimensional direction.

On the other hand, your value of the energy of a stationary mass is simply that which fits the requirement that the mass must decrease with the apparent velocity, and the energy must remain finite as the velocity increases until it approaches infinite as v' approaches c. Thus the use of your shrinkage factor fits nicely with the concept that

$$E = \frac{m_o c^2}{\sqrt{1 - \dfrac{v^2}{c^2}}}$$

when the velocity is zero and is approximately

$$E' = m_0 c^2 \left(1 + \frac{v'^2}{2c^2} + \frac{3v'^4}{8c^4} + \ldots \right).$$

This is a good approximation to the equation I derived so long as the velocities remain significantly below c, but E' would obviously be much higher than E if the values of v' were significant as compared with c. However, if the equation were rewritten

$$E' = \frac{m_0 c^2}{2} \left(1 + \frac{v'^2}{c^2} \right),$$

it would agree quite exactly with my formulation.

I do not believe any of this fourth-dimensional energy is created by conversion of mass into energy, but simply by redirecting the path of the mass from one parallel to our own motion into one which is at an angle to it. The three dimensional energy is simply a component of the total energy, $E = mc^2/2$.

If one measures the distance to object number one at a given instant in time and the distance to object number two at that same instant in time, the distance between them at that moment is exactly the algebraic difference between the two measurements. There is no correction factor required. One cannot repeat this procedure using direct measures with respect to the universal coordinate system but must perforce calculate the distance between them, taking into account the velocity of the objects. For example, were the two objects the ends of a very long yardstick, they would be calculated to move closer together at higher velocities using the shrinkage factor

$$F' = \sqrt{1 - \frac{v'^2}{c^2}}$$

By your measure, and

$$F = \frac{1}{1 + \dfrac{v}{c}}$$

in mine. So, I have used a two in the denominator of my energy equation, while granting that there may be other forms of energy involved in the mass of objects of which I have no knowledge. I have addressed only the kinetic energy.

Likewise, if one measures the velocity of object number one and simultaneously measures the velocity of object number two, the difference between the velocities is exactly the relative velocity of object number one and object number two. Again, there is no necessity to use shrinkage factors for velocity to avoid the velocity of the objects surpassing the apparent velocity of light.

In short, in reference to the local coordinate system, the universe works in perfect accord with Isaac Newton's laws without correction factors.

One final point, and I shall rest my case.

When an observer attempts to determine what a second observer sees when moving at a high speed with respect to his location, he must take into account that the second observer will consider himself to be stationary and the first observer to be in motion with respect to him. They cannot possibly observe an object at the same time by their local clocks to be in the same place. Each has his own present local time and sees everything in relation to his local clock. Even though the local observer's clocks read precisely the same time by universal standards, they differ about the position or the time of the clocks associated with everything else in the universe.

Time does not pass at different rates because the two observers are moving relative to one another, and their masses do not change as a result of the motion. One's perception of the other's time and of what the other observer sees changes—but only the perception.

So if one accepts my premise that light moves instantaneously, not at right angles to the motion of the universe through time nor at right angles to the three spatial dimensions but rather along $x - T$, $y - T$, and $z - T$ diagonals, all of Newton's laws of motion apply in this local time reference system without correction. And the best I can tell, other rather simplistic traditional rules apply as well. So there is little reason to bother trying to establish how these things would look if we made our observations in a universe where all clocks are synchronized.

EINSTEIN. We have overstayed our lunch hour! Let us make haste, or our wives will complain of our lack of appetite at the dinner hour.

I must excuse myself from further discussions today, but I am most eager to spend a bit of time recapping all you have said and adding my impressions during a brief session tomorrow morning.

MORLEY. You have been far more generous with your time than I had any right to expect, and I am most grateful.

I shall look forward to your critique tomorrow morning.

EINSTEIN. Auf Wiedersehen!

THE FINAL MEETING

MORLEY. Good morning, Albert. I hope you finished your tasks yesterday afternoon and enjoyed a good night's sleep.

EINSTEIN. Indeed, I did, although I must say that your upsetting description of a universe in which my conception of the relationship between time, space, and motion of bodies is in error left me with some wakefulness.

However, although sleep is often the best activity when there are problems to be solved, no good starting point has suggested itself.

But I think I have taken the various points you raised and tried to blend them in with my own concepts to see where they took me.

So it boils down to this. Whether the universe is physically moving through time or not, it certainly gives the impression that it is. However, this motion is not measurable with the yardstick you proffered yesterday morning. Only those things safely located in our three-dimensional world are measurable.

Things consist of physical objects and events, which may be thought of as changes in physical objects that have a very limited duration. Both objects and events can be placed in both space and time, and the measurements made define velocities. These quantities are all measurable only in reference to our three normal spatial dimensions, and of course time, which we experience only as a series of fleeting moments. We can only speculate about velocities that fall outside the normal three spatial dimensions.

I cannot accept that your very important experiments, which measured the velocity of light through space to be independent of the velocity of your laboratory relative to the sun, failed in any way. I think that you proved beyond reasonable doubt the light travels at the velocity c through space not as I defined it but as it actually is and that this can only be accounted for by the admittedly very peculiar relationship between space, time, and matter in motion.

I found your presentation most interesting and entirely consistent internally so that one cannot use one part of it to disprove another. However, just as you have questioned my definition of simultaneous events and the concept of time that is necessary in light of this definition, I must question your concept of simultaneity and the elaborate picture of the universe you have based on this definition. This requires at least a fourth spatial dimension, which lies outside our ability to investigate.

There may be some experiment that could disprove the usefulness of one of our systems over the other, but I have not been able to conceive of one. Perhaps, at some future time, as the scientific community accumulates knowledge of the details of the mechanisms of radiant energy transfer, it will become apparent which way is best.

However, at the present time, I can only thank you for a most stimulating few days of discussion and continue, as I will do, to think deeply on the subject. And by all means, continue to do the marvelous laboratory work for which I have no aptitude at all.

I do not want to discourage you from pursuing your ideas on the nature of light and the interaction of radiant energy with matter. However, the electromagnetic nature of such energy transfer seems to be established beyond question, and you yourself have attested to the finite value of light transmission through space—or at least based on the concept of time which I have carefully detailed.

MORLEY. Alas! I have once again failed to make my case. I had much the same problem convincing my colleague Albert Michelson, but he was much less interested in the actual characteristics of light and more in the mechanics of how to manipulate it.

But you have been a most courteous and attentive host, and as I have said before, I sincerely appreciate your time and attention. I know how busy the academic life can be when administrative duties are involved.

I shall continue to think on my pet obsession, as it were, but I doubt that I shall have much success in putting together future experimental projects. I am now retired from the university, and what meager laboratory I have managed to maintain privately does not lend itself to large-scale experiments.

However, my mind remains clear, thank God, and I am able to focus my attention just as well as ever, so I will do as you suggest.

EINSTEIN. Please keep in touch with me by post and let me hear any further thoughts you have on the subjects we have discussed—or any others.

A fond farewell to you, Edward. It has been a real pleasure.

MORLEY. Adieu, Albert. May you continue to break new ground as you have been doing over the past few years.

RETURN FROM ZURICH

Edward Morley returned from his European vacation and his visit with Dr. Einstein in the fall of 1910 with some disappointment. The trip had been a marvelous one, and he and Imbella had shared many delightful moments. But nearing the end of the trip, he had met with Dr. Einstein and explained to him as thoroughly as he was able that he thought, to put the matter very bluntly, that Einstein's relativity was a mistake from beginning to end. Yet when presented with Morley's explanation, which accounted for all of the observations that had been made, to his knowledge, Einstein, presumably the preeminent theoretician in the physical sciences, had politely but plainly rejected his approach.

He had learned little from Einstein, as the great physicist had not discussed his own work at all and had simply limited himself to his critique of Morley's theory.

It was now two years later, in 1912. While Dr. Einstein was enjoying considerable success in his career, Morley was comfortably ensconced in his West Hartford home and occupying his time with his garden and his collection of rocks and minerals and devoting some time to keeping up with the scientific literature, which was coming more and more to accept Einstein's approach to physics as gospel.

Einstein, meanwhile, had changed universities twice more and was now at the University of Prague as a full professor. Subsequent to their meeting in Zurich, Max Planck, the leading European physicist, had given Einstein a considerable boost in stature by declaring that Einstein's theories supported his own, which had led to the founding of quantum mechanics as a discrete branch of physics.

Morley could not satisfy himself that the increasing acceptance of Einstein's' relativity made it any more likely to be correct or his own theory erroneous. Instead, he began to look for some way to put his case forward more forcefully, but he could not think of an experiment that would differentiate between his and Einstein's relativity.

He considered a second expedition to Europe to see if the great professor might not be persuaded to at least consider his position seriously but decided against it. Einstein had, after all, politely but summarily dismissed his ideas.

Morley could not let the matter rest, for he felt that his own experimental work must contain somewhere within it the evidence that light did, in fact, move from one place and time to another place and time without traveling through the intervening time and space at all—thus making its emission and reception simultaneous events, although separated by great physical distances and long periods of time.

But how, he wondered, could he prove he was right and Einstein was wrong? Einstein himself had pointed out that he could not think of an experiment sufficient to prove or disprove the Morley approach. But perhaps somewhere in the painstaking work he and Michelson and later he and Miller had conducted there might be sufficient information to tip the scales in favor of his reasoning. His approach had never been published, and there seemed little chance of him carrying out a lengthy and costly experimental program with his current limited resources.

So, reluctantly, for a time Morley put his theory away and turned his attention toward daily routines and tasks, which were becoming more of a challenge with his advancing age.

THE LORENTZ–
FITZGERALD THEORY

Morley could not abandon his theory entirely, for he felt that it was necessary for the advancement of physics to use the simplest, clearest theory that would match the experimental results. His picture of the way space, time, velocity, and energy transfer worked was simpler and more believable than Einstein's. Einstein's equations looked more absurd to him as time passed.

One day, when leafing through his compiled papers, he looked again at the title of his 1905 paper describing the further experiments he and Dayton Miller had done. The experiments were done to substantiate the Michelson-Morley experiment, proving that the ether had no motion relative to the earth, and partly to answer critics of his and Michelson's methods. One of these criticisms had been that the luminiferous ether might have a low rate of movement but that the thermal expansion of their sandstone instrument base had obscured it.

So a part of the experiment was aimed at eliminating any possible variation in the length of the light path over which they were measuring the velocity.

Another criticism was that the there might have been a shortening of the base by virtue of the Lorentz-FitzGerald effect, which postulated that all objects got smaller along the direction of motion if they were moving at appreciable speeds compared with light.

They had, to the best of their abilities, dealt with all of these objections and found no significant change in the measured velocity of light when the direction of motion was changed. They had expected no change but had seen significance in the fact that their experiments were precise enough to have measured the Lorentz-FitzGerald shortening of their instrument path, had it been present.

The title of the paper was "Report of an Experiment to Detect the Fitzgerald-Lorentz Effect."

Of course!

After all, he had proved conclusively that, when measurements were made taking into account the motion of the earth around the sun, not only did there seem to be no drift in the luminiferous ether, if such existed, but there were several other unmistakable conclusions. One was that the presence of a significant magnetic field did not alter the measured velocity of light, and another was that the direction of motion relative to the sun did not alter the length of the apparatus used to measure the distance light traveled.

This last conclusion led to the title of the paper. The Lorentz-Fitzgerald contraction of objects did not occur under the conditions of the experiment. In other words,

$$\frac{\Delta x'}{\Delta x} = \left(1 - \frac{v^2}{c^2}\right) = 1$$

regardless of the motion of the apparatus and the laboratory containing it around the sun.

So either $v = 0$ identically, in which case c can be any value at all, or c is infinitely great, so v can have any value at all.

Now, it was obvious that, measured relative to the coordinate system of the observer taking the data, the equipment was all stationary, with essentially zero velocity relative to the coordinate system centered on his apparatus, so the velocity was close to zero. However, one does not need elaborate experiments measuring the speed of light to establish this obvious conclusion.

But as the experiments were done with the apparatus carefully aligned with the orbital motion of the earth around the sun, it was obviously the velocity with respect to the sun that was in question. This velocity, on the order of eighteen miles per second, was sufficient to make a noticeable correction with respect to coordinates on the sun.

But the Lorentz-Fitzgerald correction to the length of objects was only expected to occur when the motion was directly toward or away from the observer, so there would not have been any correction for the orbital motion even if the theory were correct.

However, suppose, instead of the sun, some other far-distant coordinate system had been selected such that the motion were directly toward it. Would not there have been a detectable contraction as seen by an observer at the origin of that coordinate system?

If the distant observer observed such a correction, Morley could testify from his own firsthand knowledge that he, the observer on the spot, saw no change whatever in the length of the optical path as the direction of motion changed with the change in the earth's orbital position. Thus, he would have to testify that if such an observer saw a change in the length of objects, it was purely an illusion, as Morley had positive first-hand data to prove there was no such change.

Thus, the conclusion could only be that the distant observer was not seeing a real change in dimension but instead was incorrectly interpreting the data because he was not correcting for the differences in the time of the measurements of the various parts of the object. There would be such differences when the data was corrected to the universal time frame of Einstein, but there would be no correction at all when using the local time system espoused by Morley.

That is, on a yardstick moving toward the observer, the observer would see the closer end at an earlier time by universal time standards than the farther end and therefore be closer to the far end than the true length. The true length could only be determined by sight by an observer moving with the yardstick.

The experiment had found the correction to be zero. So one had to conclude that when an object was moving relative to a distant observer, it did not show changes in length to an observer who was moving with the object, although it might or might not show changes in length to an observer who was stationary. In short, the stationary observer might be led to believe that the object was being foreshortened, but in fact it was not. An observer on the site of the object and moving with it had confirmed that it is not shorter.

Therefore, the on-site observer had demonstrated that the actual velocity of the object he was moving along with produced no shortening effect with increased velocity relative to anything else in the universe—but this could only be true if c, the velocity of light, was infinite.

Thus c must be the rate of motion of the universe, not the velocity of light, and the Lorentz-FitzGerald shrinking factor was an illusion brought about by using a space-time relationship based on the presumption that light moves at the velocity c.

Because special relativity agreed exactly with the Lorentz-Fitzgerald contraction of dimensions, special relativity also related to illusionary properties of space and matter.

So, thought Morley, *Dr. Einstein, I have you! I will simply publish a new interpretation of my old data with sufficient explanation that all who read it will be convinced.*

The whole concept of a distant observer moving relative to the earthbound physics experimenter deciding what was happening in his laboratory was absurd. The distant observer was in no position to issue a definitive judgment on size, velocity, mass, energy, or anything else unless he made his measurements in his local time system and converted them to the universal time system at his location. Then and only then could he make $F = ma$, and $E = mv^2/2$.

I will beat that young rascal at his own game, Morley thought. *I will do so by using one of his favorite tricks. I will describe a simple thought experiment with a result that can be reached by logic, so it will not be necessary to construct an elaborate laboratory and costly apparatus.*

By George, I think I have got it!

A LETTER TO LORD KELVIN

Morley was a careful and thorough man, and before he ventured to compose such a paper, he wished to have it critiqued by some of his learned contemporaries to make sure he was not simply carried away by his obsession with the infinite speed of light.

But who would be in the best position to give him a sound but unbiased opinion of his approach?

A few years earlier, he would have immediately chosen to report his intentions to William Thompson, who had encouraged him to conduct the experiments he and Miller had completed in 1905.

Prior to the experiments, he had discussed his thoughts at length with Thompson, or Lord Kelvin, as he preferred to be called. Thompson was a professor at the University of Glasgow and considered to be one of the leading scientific lights of his era. But just as importantly, he was an enthusiastic supporter of others whom he thought were diligently seeking the truth about the workings of the universe and was quick to applaud and encourage new ideas.

Lord Kelvin had been president of the British Royal Society at the time but had found ample time to discuss Morley's work with him during a visit to Glasgow and had encouraged him to undertake the 1905 project aimed at covering some of the criticisms of the Michelson and Morley work on the motion of the luminiferous ether. Among these was Fitzgerald and Lorentz's criticism that Michelson and Morley might not have observed the expected shrinkage of the physical dimensions of the apparatus might because the sandstone base might have expanded thermally and offset the shrinkage.

Lord Kelvin had suggested that he repeat the experiments and take pains to avoid any such problem. Without this encouragement, Morley might have let the matter drop.

Unfortunately, Lord Kelvin had passed away just a year or so ago and was no longer available to counsel him. Alas, he would have been the perfect critic, and no one else came immediately to mind. After a day or two without further inspiration, he determined to put his thoughts in order by composing a letter to Kelvin just as though he were still alive. This would help him get his arguments in order, and he might find another confidant with all of his ducks in as row, as it were.

Here is his draft of the letter to Lord Kelvin, in part:

> My Dear William:
>
> I have, since we corresponded last, seen a lot of water pass under the bridge. I should, by now, have satisfied myself with the accomplishments

of the past and left the forging into new territories to the next generation or two. However, something has been nagging at me since the work you suggested I undertake was finished in 1905.

My current thesis is very simple in concept, and I need your advice and counsel as to its soundness before I propose it publicly. I should not want to make a fool of myself dealing with such a serious matter without any physical research other than that already done to back it up.

So I ask you for an honest and unbiased critique and will take no action with regard to publication until I hear from you.

I believe that Michelson and I, and also Dayton Miller and I, established beyond a doubt that light is not conducted through space within a conductive medium, the luminiferous ether, as sound is conducted through air. We found that ether doesn't exist, or else it is stationary with respect to the earth or, more precisely, with respect to our laboratory apparatus.

Thus the light is conveyed from an emission source (our small sodium vapor lamp) through a series of mirrors and such back to a receptor surface on which we can see parallel fringes caused, presumably, by interference due to the wave nature of the light. Measurement of the spacing of the fringes gives us valuable information that has been interpreted as a result of the speed of light through space.

Now everyone seems to accept that the light moves from the source to the receptor at the value we have previously measured of around 300,000,000 meters per second and that it does not vary in speed by the least amount whether our apparatus is moving at eighteen miles per second in the circular path around the sun or turned crossways to this path.

There is no satisfactory mechanism to account for how the light makes its way through the empty space without any medium of conduction. All other waveforms, without exception, require some medium for transmission.

I theorized that perhaps what we measured was not an ordinary speed analogous to that of a speeding bullet travelling through empty space or a sound wave traveling through air but something altogether different.

I proposed that the light moves instantaneously from the source to the receptor without traversing the intervening space or time, and thus the emission and reception of a quantum of radiant energy are simultaneous events.

What then, did we measure? I believe we may have actually measured the speed at which the three-dimensional universe is moving through time, or rather through a fourth spatial dimension, which we cannot sense in any way, at the *apparent* speed of light, c. The condition necessary for this type of transfer to take place is that the light energy can only be transferred between points that lie along straight lines connecting the points that surround a receptor at the origin at a distance, *r*, such that

$$x^2 + y^2 + z^2 = r^2 = c^2 t^2 \, .$$

Such an emission source might be at a very short distance from the receptor atom at a very small time increment in the past relative to the location of the source at the present moment, or it might be as far away as a distant galaxy and many light-years away and many years in the past. It does not seem to make any difference. The energy is transferred in little packets, which Einstein calls quanta, and billions or trillions of these are required every second to account for an ordinary scenic view with our eyes.

But the mechanism, mysterious as it might be, is not the question. I simply wish to present my hypothesis in such a way as to make it palatable to the ordinary person who has an interest in physics and also to physicists and particularly to Albert Einstein. I shall do this by demonstrating that the Lorentz-FitzGerald effect, which deals with the shortening of linear dimensions in the direction of travel of very fast-moving objects, is a myth.

It is simply a misinterpretation of the data that might be taken by two observers who are moving relative to each other at velocities significant with respect to the apparent velocity of light, c.

I shall do this in the same way Albert Einstein often explains his theoretical conclusions—that is, by proposing a thought experiment in which the outcome can be derived logically so that there is no need to actually construct the apparatus and do the experimental work. The results can be derived by pure logic based on the premises put forward.

Here is a description of my thought experiment.

I imagine, on Jupiter, a duplicate of my laboratory at Case Western Reserve University in Cleveland, Ohio, and an observer much like myself conducting an experiment much as I did in 1905.

During the experiment, he observes that the speed of light does not change with the orientation of his apparatus relative to the orbital path of the earth around the sun even though the length of his apparatus should contract according to the Lorentz-FitzGerald theory, which states that objects moving at significant velocities with relationship to the measured speed of light shrink according to this rule:

$$\Delta x' = \Delta x \sqrt{1 - \frac{v^2}{c^2}} \,.$$

I observed that the object did not shrink at all with a fairly high degree of certainty. This could, of course, be because, according to my local coordinate system with its origin at the center of my apparatus, the value of v was zero. However, another possibility intrigued me. It could be because the value of c, the actual speed of light, was infinitely great, in which case a distant observer moving very fast would see the Lorentz-FitzGerald shrinkage.

Could it be possible that, instead of the speed of light being 300,000 kilometers per second, more or less, it was actually infinite? Could such a thing be possible?

When I examined my basis for these observations, I reckoned that it was quite possible. As I stood in my laboratory and carried out my experiments, I was not seeing the world through the eyes of Dr. Einstein. He defined the world at the present moment as the world in which everyone's clock displays the same universal time. I had no way of knowing if there were any other observers in the universe at the present moment by his definition of the present time.

Because, by my own measurements, light does not move instantaneously through space in his world but rather moves at 300,000 kilometers per second, I cannot see anyone else whose clock reads the present time. I can only see where they were in the past.

Yet what I am seeing at any moment in time does really comprise my world; and in this, my local world, light reaching me from whatever source, no matter how far away, is emitted at the same instant of my local time when I receive it. There is no time of transit of light in my local world.

The velocity I measured may well have been not the velocity of light through empty space but rather the velocity of my laboratory through time—or rather through a time-like spatial dimension of which we have no perception. In this local world, there is no limit on the velocity an object can reach given sufficient energy to accelerate it to that velocity. It is a very different world from that of Einstein's relativity.

Now, in my local world, when I see a moving object, I can calculate the position of the object and its velocity at the moment using c as the velocity of the universe through the time-like fourth dimension and x, t, and v as my local measurements of distance, time according to my local clock, and velocity respectively.

Using my local time coordinate system, I can see that there should be no Lorentz-Fitzgerald shrinkage of my machine, but this does not disprove the theory. Is there a way to do so?

So I imagine a researcher such as myself on a different planet in the solar system who, at the same time by his local clock (synchronized with mine), conducted exactly the same experiment and reached the same conclusions. He would also find the shrinkage in his apparatus to be zero and hopefully reach the same conclusions I did. That is, there are two ways of looking at the experimental data.

But being more intelligent than I am, he might go on to speculate that, if I existed, and if my laboratory were moving through space at a high rate of speed relative to his, then there might be such a shrinkage observed not in his apparatus but in mine! Could this be possible? Had he an unbelievably powerful telescope so that he could look into my laboratory and see my equipment, would he see it at its true length, or would it be shortened by the shrinkage factor? This would, of course, be impossible to do; but he could, if he reasoned correctly, determine the length of my apparatus by measuring the relative velocity of our two locations and using that to calculate the contraction (or expansion) factor.

So he would find that, at the same instant on our synchronized clocks when I am measuring no shrinkage at all, he is observing that my apparatus has changed in size by the factor

$$\frac{\Delta x'}{\Delta x} = \frac{1}{1+\frac{v}{c}} = 1 - \frac{v}{c} + \frac{v^2}{c^2} - \frac{v^3}{c^3} + \dots ,$$

not by

$$\frac{\Delta x'}{\Delta x} = \sqrt{1 - \frac{v^2}{c^2}},$$

and he would reach the conclusion that, while I know I made an honest measurement using my own coordinate system and found absolutely no shrinkage, he, as a distant observer moving at high velocity relative to his apparatus, perceived that his length measurement was incorrect.

But no—what he calculated was the shrinkage factor referred back to Einstein's universal time system. He must make a second correction to get what he would observe for the true length were he able to make it out through his telescope and had he an absolute system for judging length:

$$\frac{x''}{x'} = \frac{1}{1 - \dfrac{v}{c}}.$$

So the correct interpretation is that, could the second observer see my experiment in progress, by his own calculations of the length of the apparatus, it would be shortened by the factor

$$\frac{\Delta x''}{\Delta x} = \frac{1}{1 - \dfrac{v^2}{c^2}}.$$

However, were he actually able to see my laboratory, he would not see this reduction in size at all, because the yardstick lying on my worktable, and the worktable—and, in fact, my whole laboratory—would appear to have been shrunken by exactly the same ratio. Now, when one perceives an object from a distance, it is always foreshortened in the direction of the line of sight. He would not, in any way, be able to distinguish the foreshortening by comparing it with his own distant yardstick. Therefore, he would conclude, just as I have concluded, that the measurements we make in our real, everyday world are not subject to the complexities inherent in the assumptions that light moves through space at 300,000 kilometers per second and that nothing can move faster than this magic number.

What we have measured and taken as the speed of light is, in fact, the rate of the passage of time given a linear dimension. This fits all of the experiments we have made.

The Lorentz-FitzGerald correction is an artifact of our inability to accept that light is a form of instantaneous transfer of radiant energy. Einstein's theory of relativity rests squarely on this artifact, and all of the complexities of relativistic physics are likewise artifacts of a theorem that does not fit the experimental data.

William, does this make sense to you? Or do you see it as the honest but mistaken preoccupation of an old, retired chemist who has too little to keep his mind occupied?

I sincerely beg your evaluation, criticism, comments, or anything else you might think of to say on the subject.

Your faithful friend and admirer,
Edward Morley

MORLEY'S 18 CONCLUSIONS

Next, Morley sat down to draft a paper describing his imaginary experiment, which, he believed, would demonstrate that his approach to the explanation of the two time systems would convince not only Einstein but all others who had adopted relativity as the explanation for the physics of moving bodies.

It was his intention to submit it for publication by the *Proceedings of the American Academy of Arts and Sciences,* where his 1905 paper had been published originally.

Morley then questioned how many of his conclusions it might be reasonable to suggest in his paper, trying to balance, in his mind, the importance of getting his principal points across against the very real negative effect of propounding too many conclusions that would tend to antagonize readers and turn them against Morley's approach.

He wrote a list of his conclusions with an eye to trimming them down as much as possible without missing any of his fundamental ideas:

1. Light represents simultaneous transmission and reception of radiant energy, which gives the appearance of infinite velocity.

2. The measured value of the apparent velocity of light is, in fact, the measured velocity of the universe through time.

3. Time should be reckoned on a local scale, where simultaneous events are events that appear to the observer to occur at the same time.

The subsidiary conclusions were many but followed from the first three:

4. Light is transmitted from a source to a receptor only when they are properly aligned and only when the distance, Δr, and the time difference, Δt, between them are of equal magnitude.

5. Velocity, as measured by a local observer, is the local velocity of the object, and it obeys all of the commonly accepted Newtonian principles without correction.

6. The velocity of material objects through space is not limited to c, but it is unlikely that any substantial object will ever be observed moving at a velocity greater than c/2.

7. Matter is immutable and cannot be converted to energy. The mass of matter does not vary with velocity.

8. Neither time nor distance measurements change when an object moves rapidly with respect to the value of c. The relativistic shrinking factors are artifacts produced by the observer's "correction" of observed values to universal time scale values.

9. Velocity, acceleration, momentum, and energy are all relative terms and are without meaning if the location and velocity of the reference point in space and time are not specified.

There are some further speculations that might be made but for which the evidence is too ethereal to draw firm conclusions:

10. What we think of as the past is still, somehow, in existence. Radiant energy from distant galaxies continues to allow us to see them, so in some sense of the word they are still there at this moment.

11. The future, likewise, may be there already, as light transmission cannot take place without an emission source and a receptor at proper positions in space and time. Light emitted now must have a receptor available in the future to complete the energy exchange.

Morley tired of listing the conclusions and wrote a brief postscript to his letter to his deceased friend and mentor Lord Kelvin:

> So, William, I have been unable to complete any satisfactory theory of the transmission of radiant energy through space and time without the existence of a medium for transport and have concluded tentatively that light does not actually pass through empty space or through the time interval between emission and reception at all but somehow bypasses them.
>
> I leave it to future generations to provide such a mechanism but fear that the preoccupation

with relativity and the newly emerging field of quantum mechanics based on relativistic principles will prevent this from coming about in the near future.

I understand that you have theories of your own regarding the nature of space, and I would be most anxious to hear your critical comment on my proposed paper.

As always, grateful for your opinion and criticism, I remain yours faithfully,

Edward Morley

Then he put the work aside for a few days.

A VISIT WITH DAYTON MILLER

Morley did not know whom else to ask for a critical review of his proposed paper, but it occurred to him to contact Dayton Miller, the young professor at Case who had worked with him between 1902 and 1905 to construct and test the interferometer on which their 1905 paper was based.

And he did.

Miller was pleased to hear from his old friend and colleague. He was now a full professor and head of the physics department at Case and still very interested in the kinds of experiments he and Morley had performed. Aside from his accomplishments in physics, Miller was an accomplished flautist and owner of one of the world's finest collections of flutes.

After exchanging pleasantries and enquiring about Miller's musical activities, Morley got down to his reason for making the trip to Case.

MORLEY. Dayton, I have not gotten over the odd notions I had when we conducted our experimental work together. That is, there was something entirely different about the nature of light that might put all of our results into a totally different pattern. I would like to review some of these thoughts with you and see if there might not be some grounds for a bit of further cooperation.

He proceeded to spend several hours going over with Miller the gist of his theory and his proposal to expand on the possible interpretations of their results that confirmed the absence of any measurable ether velocity.

He was startled by Miller's reply:

MILLER. Edward, I am sorry to disappoint you, but I have to differ from your opinions in total.

First, I do not believe we proved that there was no ether drift and therefore probably no such thing as the ether in the first place. I believe that we simply were not using sharp enough tools to measure something so ethereal, if you will pardon the pun, as the ether.

I believe that the ether, whatever it is physically, does exist, and my belief has been strengthened by further experimentation. I took seriously the criticism that we erred in doing our experimentation in a city basement, where the surroundings and the subterranean location contributed to holding the ether more nearly stationary with respect to our laboratory than is the case when it is out there in its own natural habitat—that is, in unfettered outer space.

You suggested that we repeat our experiments on a hilltop, and I have plans to do just that, only with a much larger and more sensitive apparatus than the one we worked with.

It will be some time before my equipment is ready to test, but I have already made arrangements to perform the experiments atop Mount Washington, near the observatory but away from any other structures so as to provide the least possible interference with the movement of the laboratory through the ether.

Already, I am being attacked by Einstein, who has confessed that if my experiments show any success in identifying ether motion relative to the earth, it will completely destroy his special relativity and weaken the thesis he is working on for a more all-encompassing theory to explain gravity and, in fact, the structure of the entire universe.

You see, he is using our published results to support his special relativity theory! And I believe he is completely wrong as you do. But I must say that whether I am right and Einstein is wrong or vice versa, either way would negate your premise that light moves from place to place without passing through the intervening space.

If the ether exists, then light is conducted through it via electromagnetic radiation, and it is the velocity of the light moving through the ether we have measured. And the velocity of light through space is not independent of direction, for it will move faster in the direction of the ether drift. If I am wrong, then Einstein is right, and light is the transfer of energy by electromagnetic waves that do not require a medium to support them, for space itself has electromagnetic properties.

Of course, there is the possibility that both Einstein and I are wrong, and that you, Professor Morley, are right.

However, I strongly suggest that you hold off on your publication until I have the results from my improved interferometer atop Mount Washington before publishing your theory. If I fail to measure a consistent ether drift, then I might have to concede that your approach looks more believable than Einstein's, but I am confident that I will be able to measure the velocity of the ether relative to the earth. It should not be long.

MORLEY. Well, that is food for thought. I should have had faith in your perseverance and our common belief that the truth often lies in the smallest of details and the most concise of measurements.

I see no great harm in holding off while you complete your hilltop experiment and look forward to seeing your results.

Thank you for your time. I will be heading back to West Hartford early in the morning. Good-bye, Dayton, and good luck with your project.

Morley embarked on his trip home to West Hartford with mixed emotions. He was at a loss as to what, if anything, to do to further consideration of his theory.

Einstein had dismissed him. His chief mentor in the scientific community, Lord Kelvin, had withdrawn his advice and support by simply growing old and dying. And now his previous colleague and fellow academic at Case had rebutted him with his own previous belief that there was a real, physical luminiferous ether pervading space. The existence of the ether would overturn both his and Einstein's theories rather than choosing the correct one between the two.

Miller had scarcely listened to his thought experiment, as he believed he was going to prove the existence of the luminiferous ether, which would disprove both Morley's idea and presumably anything that could be deduced from it.

He pondered Miller's advice that he simply wait, perhaps a few years, for Miller and his co-workers to perform further experimentation to determine if Miller's theory was the correct one.

Morley was perfectly willing to embrace the existence of the ether if Miller could prove it and equally willing to embrace Einstein's point of view if there were any experimental evidence to support it over his own. But try as he might, he could not help continuing to believe that he was correct. Based on the use of the experimenter's local time to acquire all of his data, the correct conclusion was that light was transmitted instantaneously and that the data obtained in the local universe should be used as measured following Newton's laws rather than adjusted to fit the universal time concept defined by Einstein.

He would return home and continue to look for some real, physical experimental approach to prove or disprove his theory. But at seventy-two, he was beginning to feel some of the symptoms of old age, and among them was a lessening of the energy and drive he had maintained throughout his academic career.

So he would continue to ponder the problem, and unless some new thought occurred to him as to how to prove or disprove his theory experimentally, he would simply wait as Miller had suggested.

A LAST LETTER TO ALBERT

Morley reflected on the full and rewarding life he had lived and hoped he had sufficient time left to see the problem resolved. He was not able to wait without taking any action, though, and continued to follow his train of thought that Einstein and an increasingly large majority of the physics community were in serious error about the basis for Einstein's relativity.

What they must have done, he reasoned, was to use all of the measurements of physical properties as though they had actually made them in the world defined by Einstein's definition of simultaneous events: the flat plane where time was the same everywhere. However, they had actually made them in his, Morley's, world, where time was what you saw right then and everything you saw was in what Einstein would call the past.

How could this error have been so easily adopted as reality and all of the complexity inherent in physical objects shrinking as they moved faster and becoming more massive have crept into their thinking?

He pondered this question long and hard and, when he felt he had worked out a plausible answer, decided to have one more try at convincing Einstein that he had the basis for his definition of simultaneity wrong.

So he took pen in hand and began a long, long letter to Einstein to explain his reasoning.

Edward and Imbella Morley
26 Westland Avenue
West Hartford, Connecticut

Professor-Doctor Albert Einstein, Director
Kaiser Wilhelm Physical Institute
University of Berlin
Berlin, Germany

January 1, 1914

My Dear Albert:

It has been some time since our discussion in Zurich, and I regret that I have not carried out any further experimentation on the mechanics of light transmission. I must chalk this up to my advancing age and lack of youthful vigor.

You, I hear, have continued with your development of the theory of relativity and are now working on applying it to the understanding of how massive bodies are able to interact with each other at a distance so that we may ultimately have some understanding of gravitation.

Bravo! I applaud your daring in challenging the greatest mysteries of the universe.

Still, I have my fixation, if you will, on the very basis of your theory, which is now being called Relativity (with a capital *R!*). That is, as we discussed when we met in Zurich, my contention that the measurements we experimenters make are all made relative to the time we perceive as right now, where simultaneous events are those things we see at the same time.

It occurred to me that while most experimenters do not really perceive that there is a difference between these two systems of space-time coordinates, you did clearly see the difference. And I have worked out what is, in my mind, the error that occurs if the experimenters make their observations in my local system and use the results as though they were working in the universal space-time system, which they cannot do.

I have taken this rather tedious explanation and attached it as an appendage to this letter in the hope that you will find time to read it and comment if you find that I am in error.

My congratulations on your appointment as director of the Kaiser Wilhelm Physical Institute. I hope you are finding adequate time for your researches and are enjoying your location in Berlin.

With the warmest of regards, I remain your friend,

Edward Morley

Enclosure

On the Error Introduced by Failing to Differentiate Local and Universal Times

Universal time is defined as the time that exists throughout the entire universe at any given moment by a hypothetical clock at each point in space, all of which are synchronized so that any object or event that exists at an earlier time by this universal clock is in the past and any object or event associated with a later time lies in the future.

Although we all live in this universe where the present time is whatever our universal clock says it is, we are unable to communicate, in the strictest sense, with anyone or anything else at the present universal time because of the apparent finite speed of light.

Local time, on the other hand, is defined as the time at the location of a single individual observer who sees at that moment objects and events that are all at an earlier universal time that stretches into the far-distant past by universal standards.

As I pointed out during our visit, the universal time associated with any object or event seen by the observer as being in his local present has an earlier universal time associated with it, and the relationship is simply

$$t' = t - \frac{r}{c},$$

where the primes refer to the universal space-time system and the unprimed variables to those measured in the local space-time system.

The object is to analyze the error that occurs if this distinction in times is ignored and the observer uses the measurements in the local time system as though they had been made in the universal time system.

We may begin by looking at a body moving with an appreciable velocity toward an observer in the local universe as depicted in the sketch below.

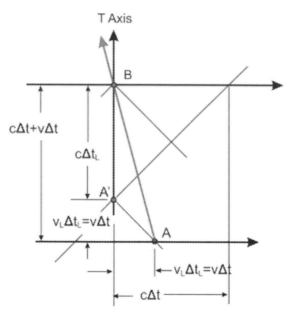

An object in motion with respect to the observer at the origin

I would like to look at the time required for the object to move a specific distance both from the standpoint of the local observer and from that of a fictional universal observer. When the object depicted is at point A, the universal observer sees it as being on the lower horizontal line, representing the x axis at universal time $t' = 0$, the starting point of the observation. The local observer does not see the object to be at point A at this time but at a later universal time, A', with the time interval defined by the distance the object will move to reach point B, which is the same for both systems. For the distance moved, Δx, to be the same for both systems,

$$\Delta x = v\Delta t = v'\Delta t' \ .$$

Because both observers see the object move the same distance, their velocities are necessarily related by

$$\frac{v'}{v} = \frac{\Delta t}{\Delta t'} ,$$

where the primes refer to the calculated values for the universal space-time system.

The relationships worked out previously for use in calculating the universal space-time velocity from the observed local distance of movement of the object and the measured local time period still apply:

$$\frac{v'}{v} = \frac{1}{1+\dfrac{v}{c}} \ .$$

From this the inverse transformation from universal to local time is

$$\frac{v}{v'} = \frac{1}{1-\dfrac{v'}{c}} \ .$$

By dividing the last equation into the previous one (which is legitimate, as both are true presumably for all values of v and v'), we arrive at

$$\left(\frac{v'}{v}\right)^2 = \frac{1-\dfrac{v'}{c}}{1+\dfrac{v}{c}} \ .$$

Multiplying both the numerator and denominator of this equation by the denominator on the right-hand side, it is apparent that

$$\left(\frac{v}{v'}\right)^2 = \frac{\left(1-\dfrac{v'}{c}\right)\left(1+\dfrac{v}{c}\right)}{\left(1+\dfrac{v}{c}\right)^2} \ .$$

At this point, there appears to be no other conclusion than that the first equation presented gives the only correct value for the velocity that should be used in the universal time system.

However, it is easy to see that if the observer does not recognize that there is a difference between the two systems, he will believe that his measurements have been made in the universal space time system to begin with. So it would appear to him that

$$\left(\frac{v}{v'}\right)^2 = \frac{1 - \dfrac{v^2}{c^2}}{\left(1 + \dfrac{v}{c}\right)^2},$$

where the values on the right-hand side of the equation are his measured values, and therefore

$$\frac{v}{v'} = \frac{\sqrt{1 - \dfrac{v^2}{c^2}}}{1 + \dfrac{v}{c}}.$$

This differs from the correct interpretation by exactly the factor

$$F = \frac{1}{\sqrt{1 - \dfrac{v^2}{c^2}}}.$$

If the velocity is in error by this factor, it is true that for a given distance covered by the moving object, the time would be in error by the same factor, and all of the relativistic values used in the universal space-time system would be in error by the same factor.

Even the distance traversed by a moving object in a given amount of elapsed time as actually measured by an observer in his own local time system would be "corrected" by

$$\frac{\Delta x'}{\Delta x} = \sqrt{1 - \frac{v^2}{c^2}},$$

which is exactly the Lorentz-FitzGerald shrinkage factor incorporated into the relativity equations.

I believe that, as I pointed out in the paper that Miller and I presented in 1905, we observed this factor to be essentially one in our experiments. That is, there was no foreshortening observed in our laboratory, nor would there be any such foreshortening in any laboratory anywhere at any uniform velocity whatever relative to any coordinate system.

I also note that

$$\frac{\Delta t'}{\Delta t} = \frac{1 + \frac{v}{c}}{\sqrt{1 - \frac{v^2}{c^2}}}$$

is exactly the expression derived when the measured values of time and distance obtained with reference to the local system are used without adjustment to represent the universal values.

In short, the shrinkage factor applied to time differences appears to be entirely due to making measurements in the local system, which is the only one actually available, and using them, without modification, as though they were obtained in the universal system.

The universal time period used for velocity measurements is always longer than the corresponding local time period for a given distance traversed, so the universal velocity is always lower than the local velocity. Misusing the local distance measurements as universal measurements causes the velocities to come out lower yet.

The one application of the shrinkage factor that is not explained is that pertaining to the increase in mass of moving objects, generally cited as

$$m = \frac{m_0}{\sqrt{1 - \dfrac{v^2}{c^2}}} \, .$$

This does not relate directly to the measurement error described for the distance, time, and velocity measurements. It comes, instead, from the postulate that nothing can move faster than c, the *apparent speed of light*. The application of a force of any magnitude for a long enough time would necessarily accelerate the mass to a higher speed, unless, of course, the mass were to increase so as to prevent it from reaching the velocity c.

I have maintained that nothing can *appear* to move faster than c when measurements are properly translated to the universal reference system, but that, when measured in the local reference coordinate system, light actually moves at infinite velocity. The velocity of massive objects obviously cannot exceed the true speed of light. The kinetic energy of masses is not limited, and the mass measured in the local universe need not increase as the universal velocity increases.

Therefore, I believe that my experimental work did, in fact, support my position that light, in a real sense, moves instantaneously through space and time and that the corrections applied to the measurements taken in the local universe of the experimenter must be corrected appropriately to produce a realistic prediction of the behavior of matter in the universal system you have defined.

While I do not suggest that you abandon the universal space-time framework for theoretical calculations, I do urge that you consider modification of your correction factor to take into account the very real difference between these two systems.

Epilogue

The letter to Einstein was either never posted or went astray in the uncertain overseas delivery system. For whatever reason, it was never answered.

Einstein continued his work, which led in the following year to the publication of what is now known as the general theory of relativity, which provides a rational explanation for the existence of gravitational forces and depicts the space comprising the universe to be curved in nature and changed in response to the presence of mass. The motion of mass is, in turn, dependent on the shape of space.

Special relativity, as Einstein's 1905 theory came to be known, was incorporated into general relativity. Both of these have come to be accepted as essentially the bedrock of modern physics, quantum mechanics, and its offshoot branches have been used to answer many of the questions that relativity did not.

Einstein, of course, renounced his German citizenship and emigrated to the United States in 1932, and he remained the world's most renowned physicist until his death in 1955.

Dayton Miller continued as head of the physics department of Case Western Reserve until his retirement in 1936. During most of this time, he continued to experiment with the use of rotating interferometers patterned after those used by Michelson and Morley and later by Morley and himself.

Dayton Miller's interferometer atop Mt. Wilson

He constantly worked to improve their design and to strive for conditions more favorable to his goal of measuring the motion of the luminiferous ether, which he believed firmly to be the transport medium for electromagnetic radiation of all kinds.

However, it was not until 1923 that he succeeded in running his tests with a new and greatly improved rotating interferometer atop Mt. Washington.

His results were widely acclaimed to be definitive proof of the existence of ether drift but also widely attacked as improperly done and poorly analyzed.

Albert Einstein followed the work Miller was doing at Mt. Wilson closely and at one point visited with him there. He was convinced that Miller's experiments, when done carefully, would verify the absence of ether drift and put the matter to rest once and for all.

When Miller reported his success in measuring the drift velocity of the luminiferous ether, Einstein was surprised and upset.

Einstein seemed worried when he wrote in 1925, "My opinion about Miller's experiments is the following ... Should the positive result be confirmed, then the special theory of relativity and with it the general theory of relativity, in its current form, would be invalid. Experimentum summus judex. Only the equivalence of inertia and gravitation would remain, however, they would have to lead to a significantly different theory."[2]

MAY DETHRONE EINSTEIN
Dr. Miller of Case to Launch New Attack

Miller was also stoutly defended, and many of the claims of critics were rebutted during the controversy over his results. However, Einstein won the popular vote, and special relativity continues to be a principle of faith for researchers. Theories contrary to its teachings are generally considered akin

---

[2] **Author's note:** This is the only factual statement in this whole presentation. It was actually written by Albert Einstein in a letter to Edwin E. Slosson July 8, 1925 (from a copy in The Hebrew University archive in Jerusalem).

to heresy. Miller seems to have been, along with the idea of luminiferous ether and ether drift, relegated to the realm of failed experiments.

But what of Edward Morley?

He outlived his wife by only a few months and died following a surgical operation in the Hartford Hospital in 1923.

There is no written record of any of the theories I have attributed to him.